A Field Guide to Identifying Unicorns
~by Sound~

Prof. OddFellow's Forgotten Wisdom

Additional funny bits by humorist Jonathan Caws-Elwitt.
Copyright © 2007 by Craig Conley. All rights reserved.

For Ken Clinger:
"nothing compares"

For Bev Yates:
"near and dear"

If a unicorn frolics in the forest with no one to hear it, then is the unicorn imaginary?
—Zen koan

If you listen to the unicorn and hear a unicorn, you've not really heard the unicorn. But if you listen to a unicorn and hear a *miracle*, then you've heard the unicorn.
—Zen parable

Contents

About This Book..9
Introduction..11

BEGINNING PRACTICE
Environmental clues..19
A faint chiming, like a distant church bell............22
An orchestral interlude..26
Sounds carried by the wind 32
A whispered voice within your mind......................36
The crisp sound of flurried snowflakes..................41
A rustling sound 48
A honeyed, tranquil sound 51
Laughter..53
Hip Heee Frr Frr..57
An ethereal melody..59
The rhythmic clip-clop of hooves............................60
A sweet, piercing voice..63
A soft crooning..65
A calm, gentle voice 68
A deep and sonorous baritone 70
A playful murmuring..73
Haughty sniffing 74
Heavy breathing..76
An echoing chant..78
A hoarse rasp..80
Strained braying..82
Humdrum humming 84
Foreign phrases..85
Weary cries..86
A magical sound 89

A terrible cry of ruin 93
A soft growling 95
A lilting voice 96
A baby's bleating call 98
A quivering neigh... 100
Cascading glissandi.. 102
Proud neighing 104
Gentle snorting 106
The bellowing wail of a mating call 108
The crunch of dry pine needles........................... 109
An alarm "sneeze".. 111
A deafening peal of thunder 112
A heart-touching sound....................................... 114
A splash of water 116
A dreadful, tree-shaking shriek of rage............... 118
A harsh braying 120
A ruffling sound... 122
A soft nicker 124
A breathy whinny 126
A slumberous sigh.. 127
The clicking of kicked-up hooves........................ 128
The sounds of grazing.. 130

Advanced Practice
Singing Whistles 135
Breathless silence 137
Deeper layers 142

Appendix: Unicorn Sound Levels in Decibels 143

About This Book

> From within the brilliance of a crescent moon,
> the silhouette of a unicorn spoke to him. The
> enchanting voice instructed him to seek the
> Child of Light.
> —Bruce R. Cordell, *Lady of Poison* (2004)

There are many ways to detect the presence of a unicorn in your own backyard, without the need for expensive electronic equipment (leave that to the greenhorn rangers) or a virgin maid (leave her to the hopeless romantics). The most obvious is via the faculty of sight. When conditions of poor visibility preclude this approach, the "third eye" of intuition is commonly employed to track down the elusive beast.

This book, however, will focus on the immense potential of the human ear. It is a little-known fact that, with listening practice, the human ear can be a peerless tool for perceiving unicorns. (The converse principle—that the unicorn ear is a peerless tool for perceiving humans—is, if true, a fact so little-known as to be undocumented.) Even those unicorn fanciers with hearing loss or profound deafness will benefit from the wealth of knowledge contained herein. Just as our old friend the blind Mexican cave fish (*astyanax hubbsi*) responds to moving visual stimuli,* the human ear responds to unicorn sounds—even to those unicornian vibrations that are technically outside the range of one's hearing.

This book weaves precious bits and pieces of evidence like a Celtic braid, gathering from a wide variety of sources: chronicles of yore, modern-day eyewitness accounts, oral histories and folk traditions, and, of course, myths and legends from around the world. These testaments are not intended to stand as scientific proof of unicorns. On the contrary, they paint a far grander picture than the tight rein of science can fabricate. It is the intention of this book to beguile your eardrums with the rhythmic hoofbeats, melodic whinnies, wistful sighs, and even bated breaths of the majestic unicorn. And when the book ends, its story will continue. For the final chapter of our saga will be yours to tell, based upon your own unforgettable first-hand experiences.

---

* Teyke, Thomas and Stephanie Schaerer, "Blind Mexican Cave Fish (*Astyanax Hubbsi*) Respond to Moving Visual Stimuli," *The Journal of Experimental Biology* 188, 89 (1994)

Introduction

> By the faint breath of movement before his face, the sudden sweet smell like the breath of a spring wind, he knew that the unicorn was nearby, invisible, watching him with wide eyes.
> —John C. Wright, *The Last Guardian of Everness* (2005)

A rustle of leaves in the breeze. A subtle creaking of tree branches. (An eerie whinny?) A humming of insects. A chirping of songbirds. (A soft clomping of hooves?)

Though they "aren't as rare as you might think,"* unicorns, like other retiring creatures of the forest, are often shrouded by their habitat. How many bird watchers have spied a warbler perched upon a tapered branch, never dreaming that the selfsame branch is, in actuality, a unicorn's horn? Truth be told, far more unicorn herds are *heard* than are ever seen. Out of the gleeful chorus of wilderness creatures, the simplest way to pinpoint an elusive unicorn is to listen for its song.

Here's a secret: expert unicorn spotters can "see" more unicorns, per capita, with their eyelids shut than the average person can see with eyes wide open.

* Phil Brucato, *Deliria: Faerie Tales for a New Millennium* (2003)

That's because they have an intimate friendship with the sounds unicorns make. As you concentrate with eyes closed and mind focused, you may detect the telltale song of the unicorn, announcing the presence of the venerable creature and beckoning you to begin your quest. When you open your eyes, the unicorn may not be immediately visible, but you'll know where to start looking.

Hearing a unicorn requires time, patience, and "deep listening" skill on the part of the human,* and vocal projection on the part of the unicorn. Because we live in a highly visual world, we rarely exercise the full range of our hearing. Yet our ears can detect things that our eyes automatically neglect. By listening as opposed to looking, we can avoid overlooking. Practice can be richly rewarding, whether one is listening for unicorns in particular or neglected delights in general.

This compact yet comprehensive guide will help you to identify the various calls of the mysterious unicorn as it frolics in its natural environment. Along the way, you will become better acquainted with unicorns' habits, eccentricities, antics, attitudes, and manners. Before you know it, encountering unicorns will become second nature to you, and you will have collected a treasure-trove of observations, anecdotes, snapshots, sketches, and memories for your unicorn scrapbook!

* Needless to say, unicorns also communicate through dreams and via emissaries (as Mary Stanton notes in *Unicorns of Balinor: Search for the Star*, 1999), but that's neither here nor there.

A few preliminary listening tips are in order:

1. Sit for a spell. Contrary to popular belief, there's no need to wear camouflage or to hide, at least as far as the unicorn is concerned. (If, however, you feel more comfortable wearing camouflage or hiding, you may do so without ill effect.) If you are still, relaxed, and "at one with nature," the typical unicorn won't be frightened. Find a comfortable place, such as under a tree, and allow yourself to "tune in" to the environment. After a few minutes, you'll notice a marked refinement in your hearing—you'll pick up on subtle auditory changes.

2. Since the human field of vision is less than 180°, there are great odds that a unicorn will approach from one of your many blind spots. Close your eyes and practice being aware of sounds coming from different directions, especially from behind you. One of the advantages of hearing over sight is that our ears offer a 360° scope.

3. Birdsong will likely be prominent in the soundscape, so practice listening beyond it to more subtle noises. Undue attention to birds when listening for unicorns is the sensory equivalent of overindulging in hors d'oeuvres and thereby spoiling one's appetite for dinner.

4. Experiment with listening at different times of day, as unicorns can have unpredictable schedules. Sunset and midnight are recommended listening times. So is the break of dawn:

> The sounds of the unicorns rose from the canyon below them as the first signs of the new day appeared in the sky. (Walter Dean Myers, *Shadow of the Red Moon,* 1997)

5. Listen for sudden changes in the sounds that come—or fail to come—from conventional animals. An animal's alarm call might warn of a predator, while celebratory sounds, noncommittal murmurings, or eerie silence might signal the presence of a unicorn. Chapter One explores environmental changes in detail. Without further ado, let the adventure begin!

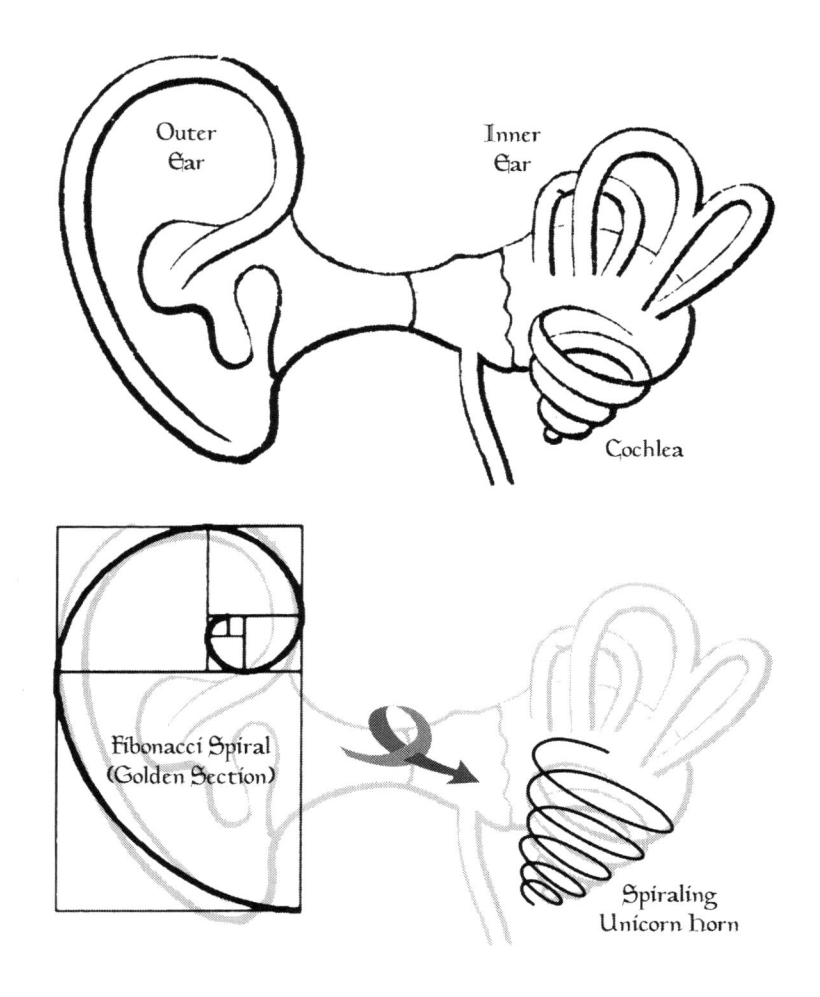

The human ear is naturally equipped to attune to the sounds of a unicorn. The outer ear follows the Fibonacci Spiral (a mathematical ratio ubiquitous throughout nature, from sunflowers to fingerprints to galaxies to unicorn horns). The spiral shape of the cochlea is the inner ear's "unicorn antenna," boosting low frequencies.

Beginning Practice

They just sat and listened to the sounds of the brook, and the rustling of the wind in the trees beyond, and the buzzing of the small flying things, and the warmth of the sun on their heads and shoulders, and the cool wet of the grass beneath, and letting their thoughts drift with the fluffy white clouds above, when they heard a whirlpool of whispering, a strange sound like they had never heard before.

And on the other side of the brook, as the sounds began to fade away, a ghostlike shape appeared, and it looked like something their mother had shown them in the old leather bound book she had kept high up on the kitchen shelf, and as one, they remembered and they said its designation, "Unicorn" in hushed tones so as not to frighten the creature that had appeared before them.

The unicorn looked directly at them, and saw them, and it spoke, with a voice like gentle bells, "You can see me."
—Silvia Hartmann, "The Golden Horse" (2001)

Listen for environmental clues.

There will be times when the natural world around you becomes aware of a unicorn's presence, even when you cannot yet perceive the majestic beast. By paying attention to subtle sonic changes, you can increase your opportunities for spotting a unicorn. Practice keeping an ear out for:

- a sudden hush of crickets
- an emphatic hoot of an owl
- a rustling of oak leaves in a grove (if oak leaves are unavailable, elm leaves may be substituted in a 2-to-1 ratio)
- a bumbling of bees
- a sigh emanating from the brambles
- an improbable tinkling of wind chimes (see next chapter)
- a pause in a woodpecker's hammering on an old tree trunk
- a whisper amid an autumnal harvest
- a melodious rumbling of thunder
- a snapping of twigs as small animals leap aside

- a whistling of the wind among the rocks
- a flatted fifth from an uninvited trombone
- a sizzling spark in the air when lightning bugs are absent

> The unicorn pranced side to side. . . . Musical voltage chimed in the soaring spaces of the forest.
> —A. A. Attanasio, *The Dragon and the Unicorn* (1996)

- a "crackling, papery sound—like the sound of a dry husk peeling from a bulb" (Carol Mason, "The Song of the Blue Unicorn," quoted in *Radical Honesty* by Brad Blanton, 1996)

The following revelatory sounds may indicate that a noble unicorn is close at hand or just around a wooded corner:

- a nibbling behind a hedge in a leafy cloister

> Hearing a noise a couple of feet away, Ruairidh threw himself behind a bush and peered through the leaves. The creature stood directly in front of his sight. He could see it bowing low and then moving its mouth as if it were talking, but he couldn't make out any noise over the rumbling from above the clouds. Then the creature pranced away to his right.
> —Sheona R. McCaig, *Scrolls of Power* (2003)

- a swoosh or swirl of air from a swatting tail

> The unicorn was calm—neck arched, heavy tail swatting lazily at its golden sides, ears

pitched forward as if it, too, were listening.
—Peter S. Beagle, *Immortal Unicorn* (1999)

- a placid munching of sweet grass

   The pure white unicorn was carefully munching at the bright green grass.
   —Katrina Patton, *A Journey into Imagination* (2001)

- a blithe chortle echoing in a soft patter of rainfall

   The unicorn whinnied like it was laughing.
   —Gail Haley, *Mountain Jack Tales* (1992)

Listen for a faint chiming, like a distant church bell.

> The unicorn head spoke in a deep yet distant voice.
> —Mary Stanton, *Unicorns of Balinor: Valley of Fear* (1999)

Have you ever perceived a silvery tinkling sound like a peal of bells reverberating from the distant horizon? That tintinnabulation may well have been the voice of an Asian unicorn gamboling about in the greenery. A unicorn of Asian origin possesses a "very musical voice quite different from that of its braying European counterpart," notes Jay Burch in *A Small Book of Unicorns* (1995). An intelligent listener will be cognizant of the differences between the two subspecies.

Bear in mind that the signature "distant" sound may not indicate physical remoteness. The ethereal, unworldly nature of the unicorn gives its voice a decidedly far-off quality. Think of it as a "special effect." The exotic reverberations evoke bygone eras, distant memories, faraway lands, remote connections, out-of-print books, and reserved feelings. Our ears pick up on that detachment and our brains try to account for it, "interpreting" it as coming from far away. Be aware that a seemingly distant chiming could indicate a unicorn right around the corner or even close enough to touch.

Here's Yasmine Galenorn's poetic description: "Her voice is that of thin glass shattering, like a hundred chimes playing in the wind" (*Magical Meditations*, 2003). Chinese legend suggests that the sound is exponentially richer; the voices of unicorns are described as being "sweet and delicate, with the sound of a thousand wind chimes" (Kevin Owens, "All About Unicorns," 2006). In one report, a unicorn "cried out in a voice like a monastery bell" (Deanna J. Conway, *Magickal, Mystical Creatures*, 2001). Another report describes "the wind chime voice of the beast" (James Pajot, *Nil Se'n La*, 2003).

Other accounts of unicorns' faint chiming in literature include:

> "Who steals the water from the unicorn's pool?" demanded a voice like chiming bells.
> —Pamela C. Wrede, *Book of Enchantments* (1996)

> "I am here," a voice said, a clean, pure sound like breath on chimes. Kara turned. The unicorn stood on the pavement not four feet away.
> —Rachel Roberts, *All That Glitters* (2001)

Church Bell Decay

Unicorn Chime Decay

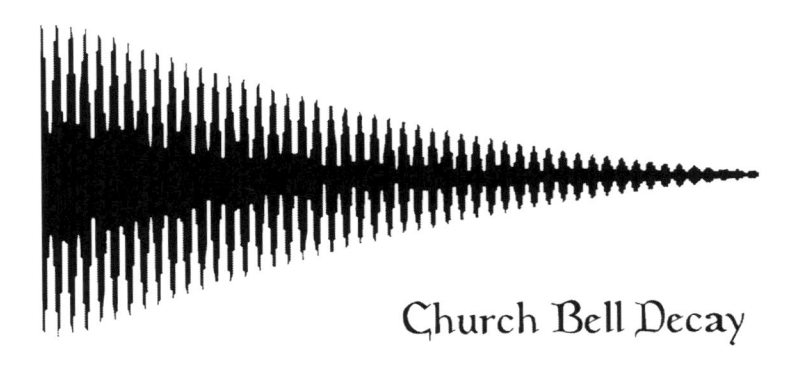

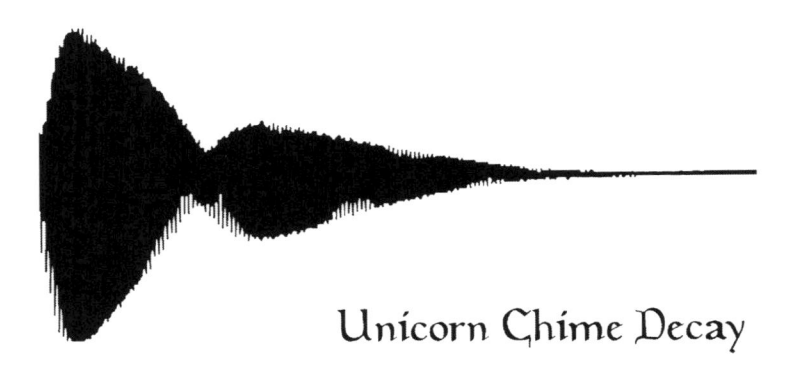

Compare the waveforms of two bell sounds. The vibrations (moving left to right through time) diminish in each, but with a difference. Notice the gradual, steady decay of the church bell. The unicorn chime, on the contrary, has an irregular decay. Its swelling waveform betrays an organic nature. Here we have two bell sounds with very different characters.

The ringing of distant church bells is a telltale indicator of unicorns, especially when no churches or bell towers are in the vicinity. When uncertain, consult a Michelin *Green Guide*.

Listen for an orchestral interlude rising above the cacophony of nature.

> I half expect to see a unicorn grazing in the patch of bright sunlight [in the sylvan meadow]. The lush sounds of harp arpeggios fade as I reenter the woods. Was it real?
> —Peter Heine, *En Route: Journals of a Mobicentric* (2000)

In his book *Unicorn Point* (1989), Piers Anthony suggests that the musical cry of unicorns has infinite variation, "each individual possessing a sound not quite like any other." Granting that "the human tongue lack[s] proper descriptions," Anthony compares the song of a unicorn to:

- "Brass" sounds
    trombone, trumpet, bugle, French horn, and tuba

- "Wood" sounds
    piccolo, violin, cello, lute, guitar, and harp

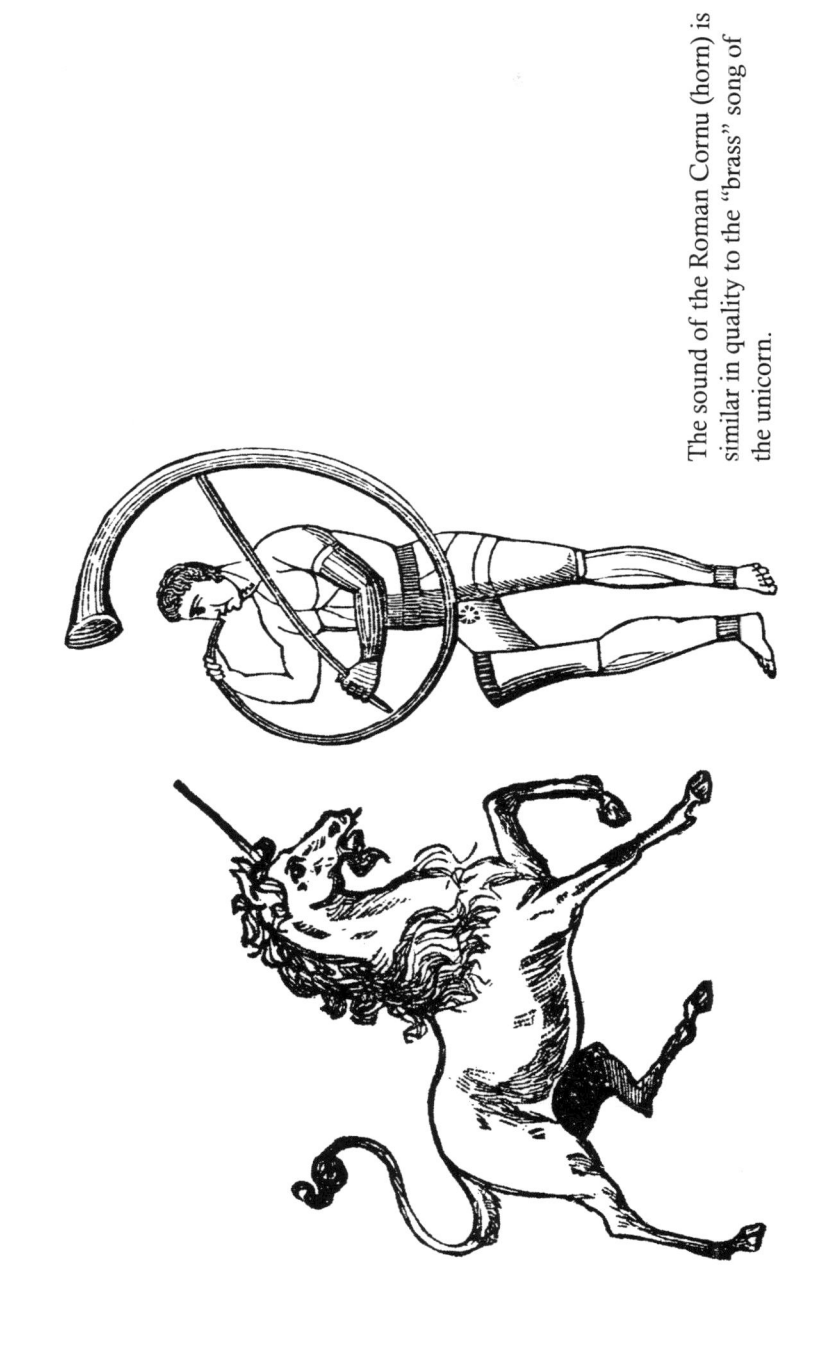

The sound of the Roman Cornu (horn) is similar in quality to the "brass" song of the unicorn.

- "Percussions"

    cymbals, bells, xylophone, chimes, and drums

- "Stray types"

    organ, music box, and piano

In his book *Cube Route* (2003), Anthony explains that unicorns sound their instruments through their horns. The reclusive sea-unicorn (commonly known as the "narwhal") similarly transmits acoustic signals through its spirally twisted tusk. "When a captive bull narwhal vocalized, strong vibrations corresponding to the sound could be felt running down the tusk" (Ted Kerasote, *Bloodties: Nature, Culture, and the Hunt*, 1994).

Unicorns' musical tones can actually form common words. In *Juxtaposition* (1982), Anthony says that unicorns "almost speak in musical notes, making them sound like *yes*, *no*, *maybe*, and assorted other words." Note that these examples of unicorn vocabulary convey the full range of opinions, and varying degrees of decisiveness, of which these complex creatures are capable.

Accounts of unicorns' orchestral voices in literature include:

> The unicorn shuddered, sending out music that filled Emily's head with fragmented and off-key chords and words that were little more than broken cries.
> —Rachel Roberts, *Avalon: Web of Magic 4: Secret of the Unicorn* (2002)

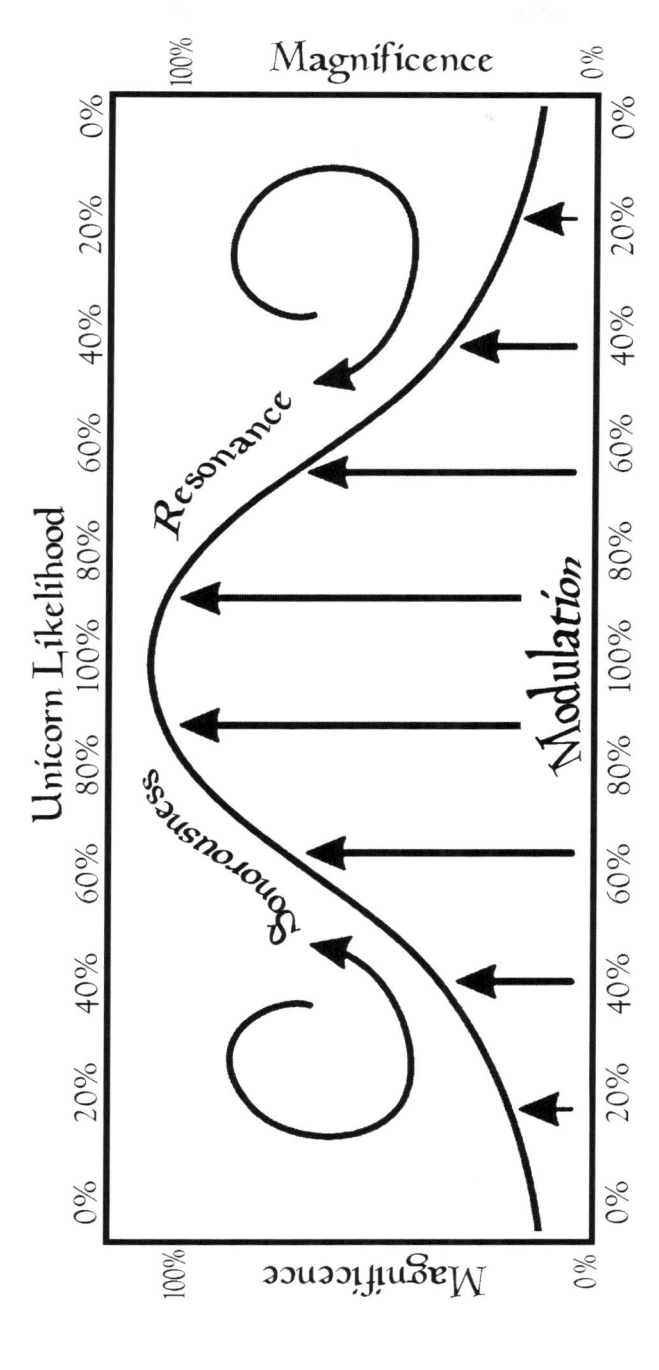

"A magnificently modulated voice spoke from the bushes.... The splendid beast snorted, the sound like the ringing of deep and sonorous bells" (Craig Shaw Gardner, *A Difficulty with Dwarves*, 1987).

The unicorn . . . made a noise: a call that went out through the night like the blast of a mighty trumpet.
—Tom Godwin, *The Survivors* (1958)

What beast has given its voice to the flute? The unicorn.
—Pamela Dean, *The Whim of the Dragon* (2003)

"Aye," the melodic tone of the horned beast sighed.
—James Pajot, *Nil Se'n La* (2003)

The unicorn spoke in a voice like a woodwind.
—John C. Wright, *The Last Guardian of Everness* (2005)

Her name was Belle, and she was a unicorn. She spoke to me musically on her horn.
—Piers Anthony, *Phaze Doubt* (1990)

At last the unicorn spoke. Its voice was clear and piercing, like the sound of a flute.
—Pamela Dean, *The Secret Country* (2003)

The shimmer of blue light changed to an emerald green and [there] stood a brilliant white unicorn. It spoke in a rhythmic voice.
—Michele Avanti, *GreeHee* (2006)

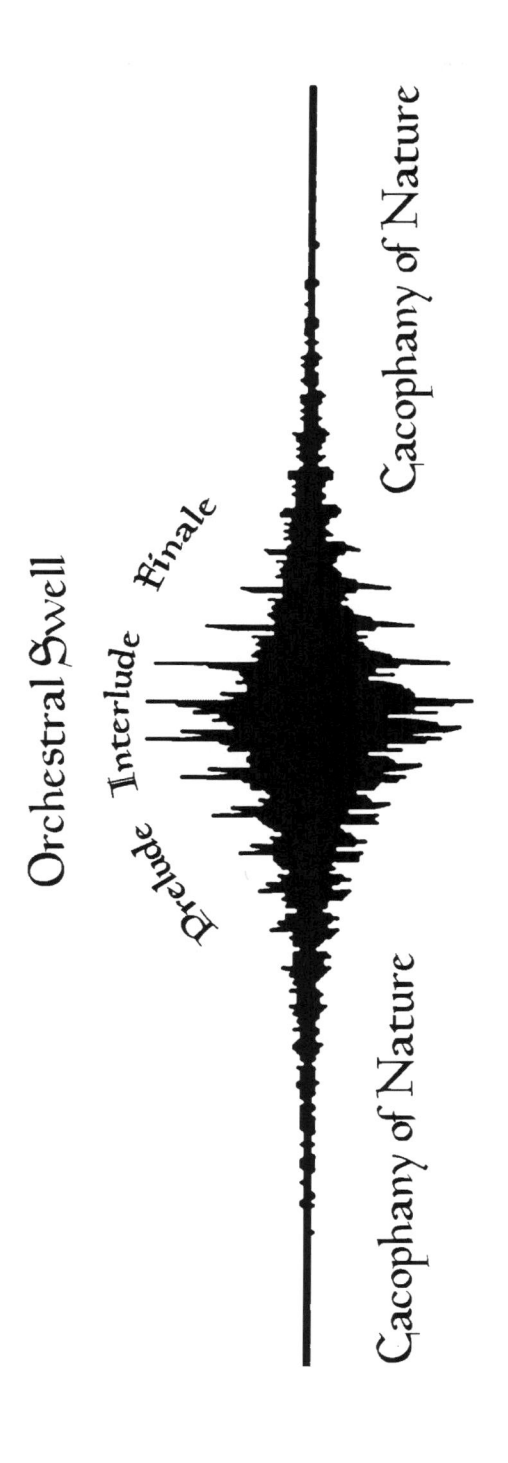

In this waveform, a unicorn's orchestral interlude swells above the cacophony of nature.

4

Listen for sounds carried by the wind.

> Another unicorn's call came to him on the wind.
> —Hasüfel, "Alma's World: The Far Plains" (2004)

If not distorted by foliage, a wind gust might carry fragrances from afar, winged seeds, the moans of trees, echoes of laughter and distant whistles, the howls of storms, sudden chills, the invocations printed on prayer flags, and the sounds of a gamboling unicorn. It is common knowledge that unicorn sound waves can be better detected downwind of the beast than upwind. But why is that, considering the fact that wind velocities are a mere fraction of the speed of sound (750 miles per hour)? Dr. James B. Calvert, Associate Professor Emeritus of Engineering at the University of Denver, suggests that the phenomenon may derive from wind shears deflecting sound waves either downward (more toward the listener) or upward (away from earshot):

> When a wind blows, it is retarded at the surface—a sort of boundary layer effect—and increases in speed aloft. This is a wind shear. ... A wavefront propagating with the wind will have its top inclined forward, so it will tend to return to the surface, while a wavefront propagating against the wind will be deflected upwards. ("Sound Waves," 2000)

Naturally, if a unicorn sound is carried by the wind, the source of that sound will be upwind (opposite the direction of the gust). In the case of whirlwinds, anything goes.

Accounts of unicorns' wind-swept voices in literature include:

> She speaks in a gentle voice like wind whispering through the trees.
> —Rikale Fyrlight and Kalika Kiskmet, "The Pool" (2006)

> The wind carries their voices—away fly the sentences like narrow ribbons.
> —Katherine Mansfield, "The Wind Blows," *Bliss, and Other Stories* (1920)

I thought I almost heard a unicorn lullaby in the air.
—Tanathir, *North of the Palace* (2006)

Neighing far off on the haunted air
The unicorns come down to the sea.
—Conrad Aiken, *Senlin* (1925)

"You have two options," the unicorn head said. Its voice was tinny in the dry desert air.
—Mary Stanton, *By Fire, by Moonlight* (1999)

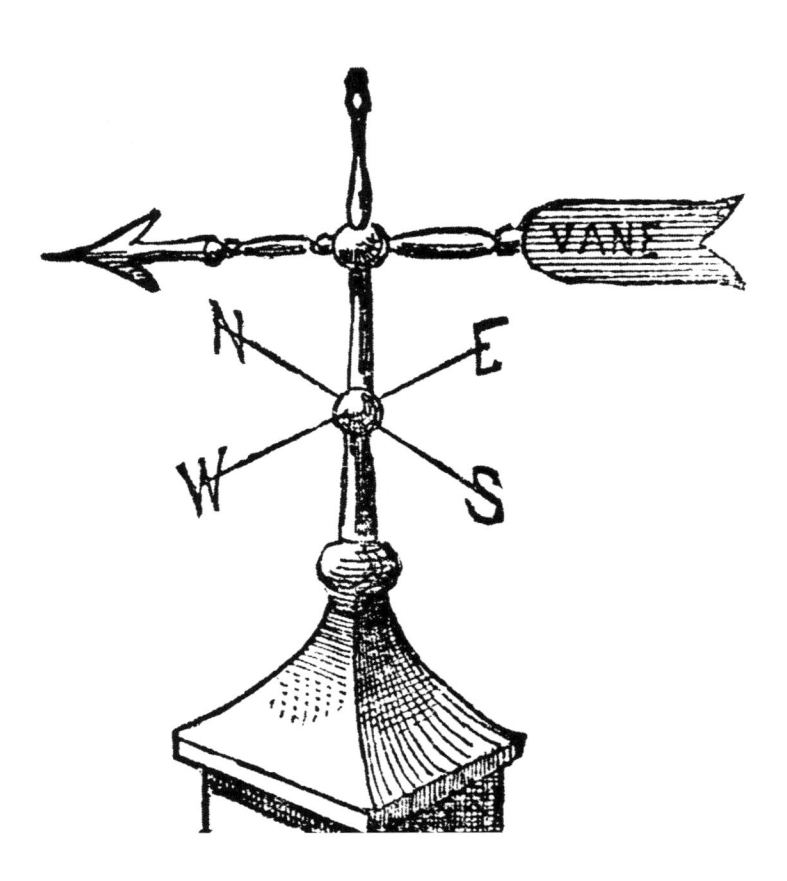

Weaving in with the serene sounds is another song, a whisper so soft that it seems to be the breeze. However, sharp ears may be strained to catch the wisps of a voice, the words muffled in some melody. The song fades away on the wind as a brown unicorn daintily steps forth from the trees.
—Samantha Schwarte, "Crystal Unicorn" (2005)

Fari heard something on the wind, lifted his head and looked into the distance. He couldn't see anything, but he knew something was nearby. . . . Sensing something behind him, he suddenly turned round to see a small unicorn that had approached silently and was looking at him over the fence.
—Geoff A. Rigby, "A Magical Meeting" (1996)

Before the harmonies were broken, unicorns and winds danced together with joy and no fear.
—Madeleine L'Engle, *A Swiftly Tilting Planet* (1978)

In this waveform of a unicorn sound carried by the wind, notice the sudden gust (the "horn") and gliding movement at the end.

Listen for a whispered voice within your mind.

> Instantly, he realized that she had heard his thought. And then, in a full, whinnying voice, she spoke directly into his mind.
> —T. A. Barron, *Shadows on the Stars* (2005)

The telepathic ability of unicorns is legendary. As described in Serena Carrington's *Avalon* (2002), a unicorn's gentle voice is often heard as if within the listener's head. Similarly, in *Emerald Sword* (2002), J. M. Sampson refers to a unicorn's "mind-words." The effect is at once soothing and startling.

On occasion, mind-words of a single unicorn may sound like many voices speaking simultaneously. Peter David explains in *Fall of Knight* (2006):

> He heard the beast's voice inside his head. It sounded both old and young at the same time, and even though it was one voice, it sounded like many. Like a hundred, no, a thousand voices speaking in concert.

37

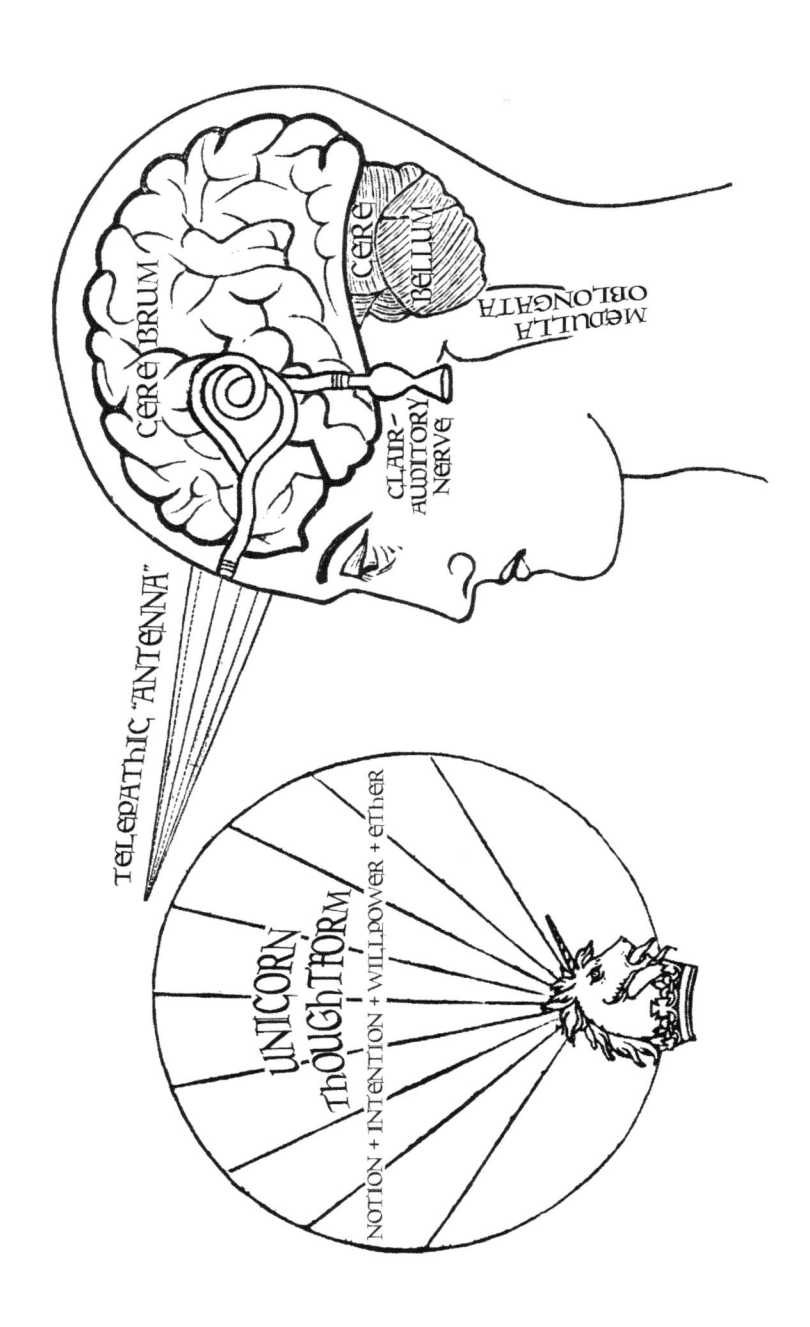

The mind-words of several unicorns in unison can become a veritable cacophony:

> The creatures started babbling, then shouting, and the unicorns whinnied madly until Lily could hardly hear a thing for the rumpus in her head.
> —Natalie Prior, *Lily Quench and the Magician's Pyramid* (2004)

Mental whispers may seem:

- like an attempt to whistle
- ever so brief
- confidential
- delicate as thistledown
- familiar
- like a falling feather
- encouraging
- like rain on leaves
- faint
- like a soft blowing
- heavenly
- like a steaming teapot
- peaceful
- like a sleepy sigh
- lulling
- gentle
- soothing
- like a voice from the grave
- enchanted
- husky
- like a rustling wheatfield
- hollow
- like something from ancient times

- like rough cloth brushing along a dusty surface (Rebecca Bradley, *Scion's Lady*, 2000)
- caressing

> Then she noticed the rustling inside her head. A caressing sound like the sough of leaves falling on a table of crystal glass.
> —Jude Chance, *Whisper of Angels* (2005)

- like bubble bath
- like the "wailing of some lost soul" (Arthur C. Clarke, *2010*, 1982)
- like "an ancient, common tongue" calling one back to a communion once shared long ago (Robert Romanyshyn, *The Soul in Grief*, 1999)

Accounts of unicorns' mind-words in literature include:

> My unicorn can whisper strange things when I want him to, and sometimes when I don't.
> —Larry Niven, *More Magic* (1984)

> Seize my horn, said his soft voice in her head.
> —John Grant, *The Far-Enough Window* (2002)

> The unicorn's eyes narrowed and she heard his Voice echo in her mind again.
> —Mark Keavney, *The Archer's Flight* (2005)

> The unicorn's "voice" was more thought than vocal sound; but she imagined that the timbre approximated that of a bard she heard once in the Great Hall . . . a sweet tenor's tone.
> —Lrd Kedryn, "Visions of Beauty," *Neverwinter News #163* (1996)

They do speak, sir, although not with words.
The unicorn sent her thoughts right into my
head. I understood her meaning.
—L. E. Engler, *The Forgotten Isle* (2004)

A soft gentle voice whispers in your mind as
if carried by the breeze passing through the
gentle grove.
—Pharos, "Crest of the Unicorn" (2004)

"I can hear a voice in my head, and it must be
him." He pointed at the unicorn.
—John Peel, *Book of Magic* (2004)

I cry to the unicorn in my mind; but though he
hears me, he seldom answers.
—S. P. Somtow, *Tagging the Moon* (2000)

6

Listen for the crisp sound of flurried snowflakes.

> As I hear the peaceful sound
> of snow falling on snow,
> my soul slowly softens.
> —Robert J. Wicks, *Snow Falling on Snow* (2001)

The wispy sound of glittering snowflakes gently falling to earth—one unicorn listener likens it to "the whisper of angel wings." That faint sound is subtle but by no means imperceptible. The key is to distinguish it from total silence. Barbara Wright explains: "the lovely sound of snowfall" is "no sound at all, really, but neither [is] it silence" (*Plain Language*, 2003). Sandra Meek agrees, but adds an intriguing qualifier: "No sound for snow, no definition of ice. The unsaid among shuttered wings" (*Nomadic Foundations,* 2002). Without question, unsaid utterances can resound in the silence between two beings. Perhaps they are unspeakable. Perhaps they are ineffable. In any case, they spiral, grow, and ring in our ears. As Mary Summer Rain has noted, deep silence intensifies the sound of falling snow (*Soul Sounds*, 1992).

Pointed Projections

A – Snowflake Dendrite
B – Unicorn Horn

The delicately complex sound of snowflakes can connote anything from serenity to ominousness, depending upon the unicorn's intentions. Donna Andrews records "the eerie, muffled sound" of snow (*You've Got Murder*, 2002), while Judith Hendricks offers a more endearing description of "the soft, purring sound of snowfall, like a big cat." She adds, in paretheses, "Yes, there is a sound, but you can only hear it in absolute silence" (*The Baker's Apprentice*, 2005). Indeed, according to professional sound designers Deena Kaye and James LeBrecht (*Sound and Music for Theatre*, 1999), the sound of snow has a broad range:

- calm
- menacing
- comforting
- threatening
- inviting
- foreboding
- soothing

It should come as no surprise that unicorns make a sound like falling snow, for snowflake crystals and unicorns share many characteristics:

- no two alike
- sparkly white in color (having absorbed all of the surrounding sunlight or moonlight)
- difficult to predict
- beautiful
- symbols of purity
- natural materializations
- symbols of innocence

- can be dangerous at times
- symbols of serenity
- excellent insulators
- ephemeral
- blend into the landscape

Intriguingly, freshly fallen snow can actually *store* the sounds of a unicorn as well as project them with clarity. A carefully gathered snowball is like a library of sounds stored on crystalline shelves. When held to the ear like a seashell, it may whisper the unicorn secrets it has absorbed. Ergo, composer and music theorist John Rahn describes "a little snowball of sounds" (*Perspectives on Musical Aesthetics*, 1995). Snow expert Nancy Armstrong explains that "When snow is newly fallen, sound waves are absorbed into its soft surface. Later, when the surface has hardened, sounds may travel further and sound clearer, because the snow reflects sound waves, sending them more quickly through the air" (*Snowman in a Box*, 2002). Barbara Blair concurs: "snow is a wonderful substance to enhance awareness" (*Communing with the Infinite*, 2006).

In his poem "Snowdrift," Tony Sanders provides a practical description:

> Listen.
> The sound of the snow falling
> is the same as the sound of creosote
> spluttering in the stove pipe.
> (*Partial Eclipse*, 1994)

The imagist poet Kim Kwanggyun offers an equally mundane yet highly evocative description; he compares the sound of snowfall to "the swishing of a woman undressing" (Peter H. Lee, *A History of Korean Literature*, 2004).

The suggestive sound of snow can also be:

- divinely musical

    > Professional trainer Steve Ilg calls snowfall "a form of divine music" (*The Winter Athlete*, 1999).

- like a whimpering specter

    > What weeping ghost
    > inside the sound of
    > snow is diminished?
    > —T. Byron Kelly, *Project End Of Days* (2005)

- like sieved flour

    > When fine flour is being sieved, it falls lightly to the floor without a sound; snow falls just as silently.
    > —Pandita Ramabai, *The Peoples of the United States* (1889)

- astonishing

    > The most astonishing one for me is the sound of snow falling.
    > —Maureen Smith, *Full Tilt Living* (2001)

- dreamy

    > Dream sound. Snow.
    > —Hayden Carruth, *Collected Longer Poems* (1993)

- enlightening

    > The Zen master Hakuin said he "gained an enlightenment from the sound of snow falling" (*The Zen Master Hakuin: Selected Writings*, translated by Philip B. Yampolsky, 1971).

- dry, like sand running over paper (Mark Mergemann, "Letter From Nuiqsut," *Alaska Passages*, 1997)
- peaceful
- glassy
- like spilling sugar
- persistent
- hollow
- pattering
- slithering
- tickling
- drumlike
- hissing
- swooshing
- wailing
- forlorn
- scraping
- feathery
- gently caressing
- scratching
- faintly ticking

Like a vein of ice crystals, this is the delicate waveform of a unicorn's subtle snowflake voice.

- isolating
- bright
- monotonous
- rustling
- fierce
- softly sputtering
- eloquent
- enveloping
- whispering
- miraculous
- cleansing

Accounts of unicorns' snowflake voices in literature include:

> The unicorn made a sound like falling snow, out of wonder and maybe fear.
> —Callie Richardson, "Where Unicorns Go" (2005)

> Then she heard a tiny sound. And felt a warm, silky touch on her shoulder. She realized that it was the unicorn.
> —Emily Rodda, *Fairy Realm 6: The Unicorn* (2004)

7

Listen for a rustling sound.

> A rustling of leaves,
> I hold my breath,
> ready to face the
> impossible.
> —Suzanne Delaney, "Unicorn Hoofprints" (2001)

Beautiful to the human ear, rustling sounds are typically caused by stealthy movements and rubbing. Rustling sounds are various in tone:

- brushing, like a broom sweeping away cobwebs
- hissing, like a fierce whisper
- soft and muffled, like a blanket or thick rug
- crackling, like leaves or dry grass, or kindling catching fire
- fluttering, like the wings of frightened birds
- crumpling, like a scattering of parchment on a composer's cluttered piano, or someone stepping on a paper doll
- brief and slight, like toffee wrappers
- scraping, like razors on skin
- popping, like static electricity

Causes of Rustling

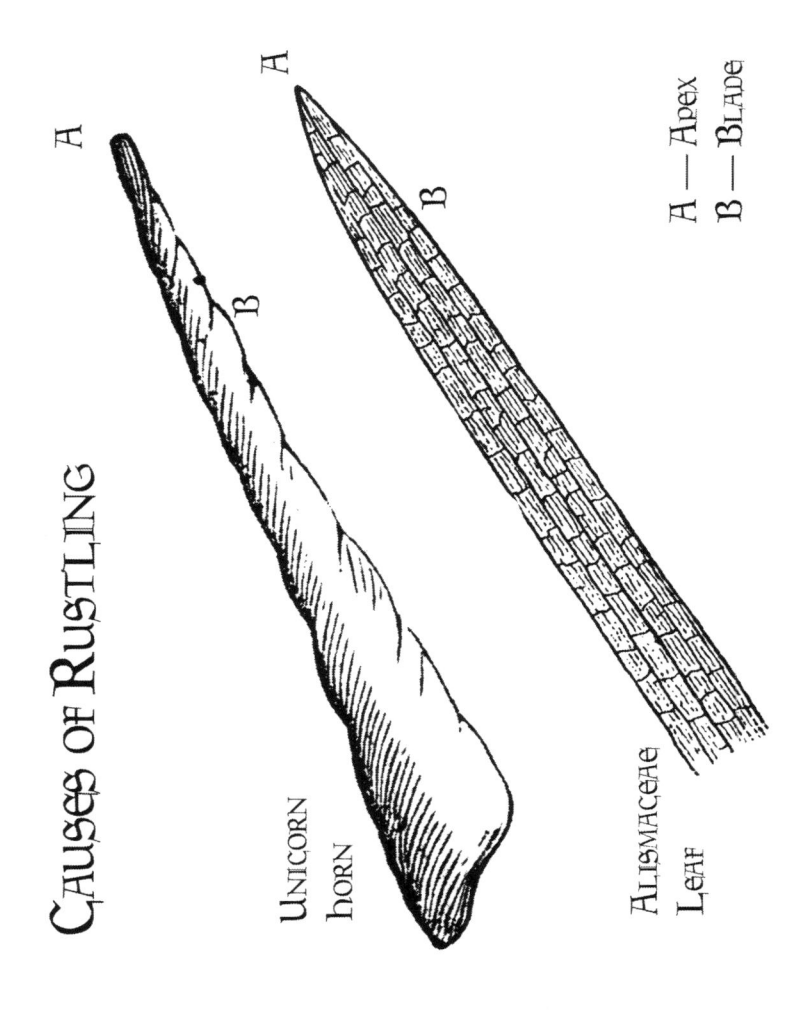

Unicorn Horn

A — Apex
B — Blade

Alismaceae Leaf

- prolonged whooshing, like blowing air into a balloon
- sputtering, like steam from a leaky boiler
- sighing, like sand slipping through one's fingers
- heavy, like the pages of the Sunday newspaper
- waxen, like the unwrapping of a sandwich

Accounts of unicorns' rustling voices in literature include:

> Perhaps it was just the rustling of the leaves, but a voice seemed to say, "Don't leave Elysia. Stay . . . we need you."
> —Kathie Billingslea Smith, *The Enchanted Unicorn* (1987)

> There was a rustling in the thick bushes and the unicorn burst through.
> —Terry Pratchett, *Lords and Ladies* (1992)

> There was a rustle across the way. . . . On the other side of the stream a unicorn had stopped to drink.
> —Kestrelsan, "In the Morning" (2003)

> In the forest not far from here I found a large hollow tree filled with dead leaves. As I began to make a bed for my child among the dead leaves, I heard a rustling and found a nest of fawns. They had been so well covered in leaves that I didn't see them until they moved. Each fawn had a tiny horn in the middle of its brow.
> —Nigel Suckling, "King Arthur and the Unicorn" (1996)

8

Listen for a honeyed, tranquil sound.

> The unicorn sidled around to face me. Her voice, even under stress, had a mellifluous quality, soothing as a mother's—or a lover's.
> —J. A. Erwine, *Wondrous Web Worlds, Vol. 2* (2002)

The mellow, sweet-sounding, liquid voice of the unicorn is unmistakable, as it radiates pure love. Horse expert Adele Von Rust McCormick notes that like "its ancestor, the unicorn," the Classic Horse "is imbued with the same magical qualities." Both animals awaken the human heart "to the essence of a love the ancient Greeks called *agape*—a complete and all-encompassing love of the creator and the created, a love difficult to practice as it is so selfless. Yet we can grow closer to it if we listen to the voice" of these alluring animals (*Horse Sense and the Human Heart*, 1997).

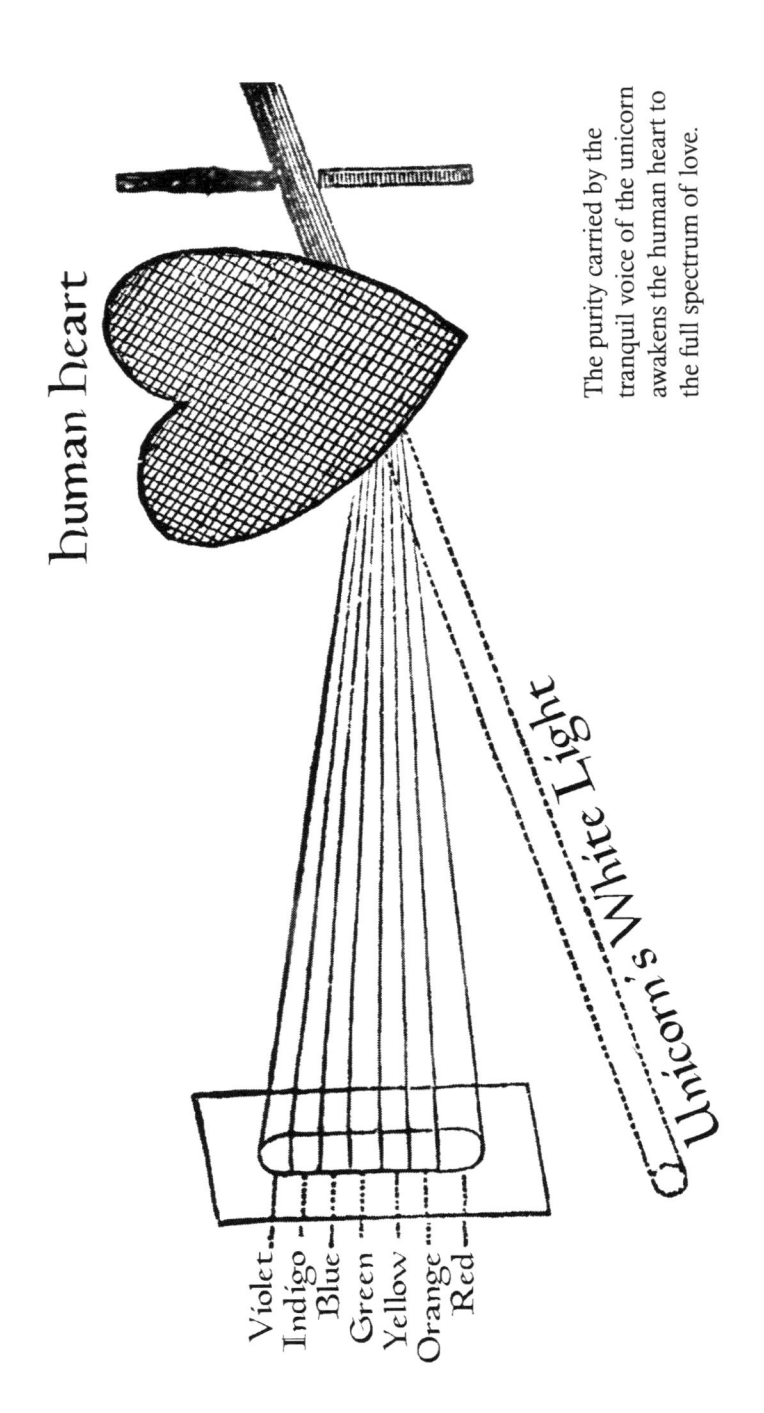

human heart

Unicorn's White Light

Violet
Indigo
Blue
Green
Yellow
Orange
Red

The purity carried by the tranquil voice of the unicorn awakens the human heart to the full spectrum of love.

9

Listen for laughter.

> The unicorn considered him with a large, purple, dubious eye; but when it spoke, it sounded on the verge of laughter.
> —Pamela Dean, *The Whim of the Dragon* (2003)

"The unicorn laughs," notes Yasmine Galenorn (*Magical Meditations*, 2003). Unicorn laughter is essentially a form of vocalized panting, with spasmodic bursts of air. Speech expert Evangel Machlin explains:

> The contractions which are both the cause and effect of laughter are identical with those of panting. The diaphragm contracts lightly, quickly, rhythmically, sending out puffs of breath which have the familiar 'huh-huh' sound. These puffs are nearly voiceless, and a great many can be produced between one inhalation and the next. They sound almost exactly like laughter. (*Speech for the Stage*, 1992)

But just as an ability to distinguish between laughing and panting can be crucial in the course of human relations, an ear for the difference between these two sounds will stand the unicorn seeker in good stead.

With its lingering echoes, vocalized unicorn laughter may be heard up to three miles away. Its tone varies:

- strangely playful
- like chuckles from within a hall of mirrors
- silvery, like tinkling wind chimes or breaking glass
- primal, perhaps even eerie
- rich and warm
- high-pitched, piercing
- low whinnying
- dry
- like wet pebbles tumbling down a hillside
- joyful, ebullient
- deep growling or snarling
- staccato
- mocking
- spontaneous
- wild and wonderful
- bubbling over, as if water has gone up one's nose
- hollow moaning
- rapid fire barking

Voiceless unicorn laughter is akin to Franz Kafka's description of "the sort of laughter that can be produced without lungs. It sounds something like the rustling of fallen leaves" ("A Country Doctor," 1919). Like the bonobo, voiceless unicorn laughter "sounds like the laughter of someone who has laughed so hard that he has run out of air but can't stop laughing anyway" (Sue Savage-Rumbaugh and Roger Lewin, *Kanzi*, 1996).

In *Juxtaposition* (1982), Piers Anthony describes a unicorn's "blast of musical laughter." Other accounts of unicorns' laughing voices in literature include:

> The unicorn's laughter, loud and rambunctious, created chaos in the creek.
> —Marcus Rose, *Natural Roses* (2000)

> And when the tail of the unicorn brushed the little ones, they gave off little notes and chimes, and sometimes even a sound like a child's laughter.
> —Tanith Lee, *Red Unicorn* (1997)

> Then she put her arm around its neck and hugged it, and it didn't seem to mind because it whickered softly, as if it were laughing.
> —Pamela Freeman, *The Willow Tree's Daughter* (1998)

> Another Unicorn glanced at him and laughed.
> —Robert O'Finioan, *Innocence Turned Deadly* (2002)

The waveform of unicorn laughter reveals a lively spontaneity.

He made a sound somewhat like a chuckle, and rubbed his hoof against the soil in a gesture meaning, "Come here."
—Tomorrow, "A Far Away Union" (2006)

The unicorn makes a sound that is almost like a laugh and then turns and begins to gallop away.
—Ryan Moore, "Ars Magica: Negrath Saga" (1999)

Listen for these joyful sounds: hip heee Frr Frr and Bree-hee-hee.

The distinctive, joyful neigh of a unicorn—*hip heee frr frr*—is described by Umberto Eco in *Baudolino* (2000):

> she said o my god now how will we make the unicorn come and just then I heard a voice from Heaven said that the unicorn *qui tollis peccata mundis* was me and I started jumping around the bushes and crying *hip heee frr frr* because I was happier than a real unicorn because I had put my horn in the virgin's lap and this was why Saint Baudolino had called me son *et setera* but then he forgave me and I caught site of him other times but only if there is plenty of fog or if it isnt bright like to scorch everything.

What do the joyful neighs of a unicorn *mean*, exactly? In his philosophical essay "The Crown" (1914), the great English writer D. H. Lawrence transcribed "the voice of the unicorn crying in the wilderness." Following is the unicorn's profound, eternal message:

> Behold, I am free, I am not enveloped within this darkness. Behold, I am the everlasting light, the Eternity that stretches forward for ever, utterly opposite of that darkness which departs backward, backward for ever. Come over to me, to the light, to the light that streams into the glorious eternity. For now the darkness is revoked for ever.

Indeed, the voice of the unicorn has the uncanny power to dispel the darkness. In *Dragons of Autumn Twilight* (2003), Margaret Weis describes it in this way:

> Even as the deep voice spoke, the darkness parted. A gasp of awe, gentle as a spring wind, swept the company as they stared before them. Silver moonlight shone brightly on a high rock ledge. Standing on the ledge was a unicorn. She regarded them coolly, her intelligent eyes gleaming with infinite wisdom.

Like Lawrence, C. S. Lewis described the joyful cry of the unicorn—*bree-hee-hee*—and summed up its eternal message:

> I have come home at last! This is my real country! I belong here. This is the land I have been looking for all my life, though I never knew it till now. . . . Bree-hee-hee! Come further up, come further in! (*The Chronicles of Narnia: The Last Battle*, 1956).

11

Listen for an ethereal melody.

> The unicorn sounded a brief melody.
> —Piers Anthony, *Phaze Doubt* (1990)

Unicorns sometimes hum a soft, ethereal song that seems familiar at first but then fades into oblivion. One is reminded of Edgar Allan Poe's description of a voice "like the spirit of a departed sound" ("Berenice," 1835).

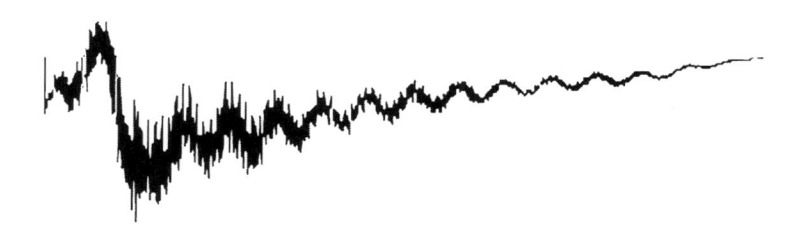

This stunning waveform depicts a unicorn's ethereal intonations fading into oblivion.

12

Listen for the rhythmic clip-clop of hooves.

> If unicorns spoke words while running, they would be excellent at poetic meter, for their hooves would measure the cadence.
> —Piers Anthony, *Split Infinity* (1980)

Margaret Mallett, in *The Primary English Encyclopedia* (2001), suggests that the galloping of unicorn hooves sounds like coconut shells. However, it will be more realistic to expect a subtler vibration (unless you have chosen a tropical location for your unicorn encounter, in which case the sounds you hear when the beast's hooves connect with the turf may actually *be* coconut shells). Husks aside, consider this more subdued example:

> The sound of his hooves against the stony floor of the cave was like distant silver bells.
> (Bruce Coville, *Into the Land of Unicorns*, 1994)

Consider, too, this account of a soft, muffled sound:

> Behind us, the unicorn canters; I can hear the hoofclacks on the concrete, not a clippety-clop

of an ironshod horse, but a softer sound. It is almost the sound of raindrops on the leaves of a banana tree. (S. P. Somtow, *Tagging the Moon*, 2000)

Interestingly, the sound of unicorn hooves can be muffled even by a mere absence of light:

> The only sound was the steady rhythm of the unicorn's hooves, and even that seemed somehow muffled by the unrelenting dark.
> —Simon Green, *Blue Moon Rising* (1991)

Janny Wurts hears in those rhythmic clip-clops no less than echoes of nobility:

> Exalted form spoke in the purity of tossed manes, and high tails, and in the stone hooves of the unicorns, dancing. (*Traitor's Knot*, 2006)

Other accounts of unicorns' clip-clopping hooves in literature include:

> In a long moment, there was the sound of galloping hoofs. Then a unicorn stallion appeared.
> —Piers Anthony, *Question Quest* (1991)

> Behind them the sound of hooves drummed on the grass; the unicorns raced away into the darkness.
> —Sherwood Smith, *The Emerald Wand of Oz* (2005)

> They followed the clip-clop of the unicorn's hooves.
> —Danielle Peak, *The Enchanted Conquest* (2003)

He hadn't got much past the edge of the orchard when he heard the unicorn a-coming. It was moving so fast it sounded like a big wind blowing up. The rumble of its hooves was like summer thunder.
—Gail Haley, *Mountain Jack Tales* (1992)

The unicorn turned, its head low, and started walking the path back down the mountain. Dersil watched it go, listened to its hooves on the rough stones. Tac, tactac, tac. There was a song in everything, Dersil knew that, but this song was the slow minor of life. There was no melody in those hoof beats, only monotone. No rhythm, only repetition.
—Mithandir, "The Grey Unicorn" (2005)

He listened to the unicorn's hooves, but he did not turn to watch it go.
—Will Shetterly, *Peter S. Beagle's Immortal Unicorn* (1995)

13

Listen for a sweet, piercing voice.

> Lost in the hypnotic eyes of the unicorn, he
> heard a sweet and primeval voice in the air.
> —Ben Okri, *Astonishing the Gods* (1999)

Mary Stanton records hearing the singular voices of unicorns frolicking on a riverbank:

> And the sounds—the high sweet voices of the unicorn foals who played by the Imperial River, the singing of two mares in a happy duet, the bell-like splash of water! The sounds were like nothing she had heard before. (*Night of the Shifter's Moon*, 2000)

L. Frank Baum is less poetic in his description of a unicorn's "high, squeaky voice" (*The Magic of Oz*, 1919). In any case, unicorns' pristine, piercing voices seem to hang in the air. They may be reminiscent of:

- squeals of delight
- spears of light gliding through the darkness
- air escaping a balloon
- sleigh bells

- "amazing grace"
- the Bee Gees

Accounts of unicorns' sweet, piercing voices in literature include:

> This last night, when the moon was nigh but full, I chanced to hear the clarion call of the unicorn.
> —Shantell Powell, *The Virgin and the Horn* (1998)

> "The Lords of the Dead," said the piercing voice of a unicorn, from the froth among the trees, "Have been sleeping."
> —Pamela Dean, *The Whim of the Dragon* (2003)

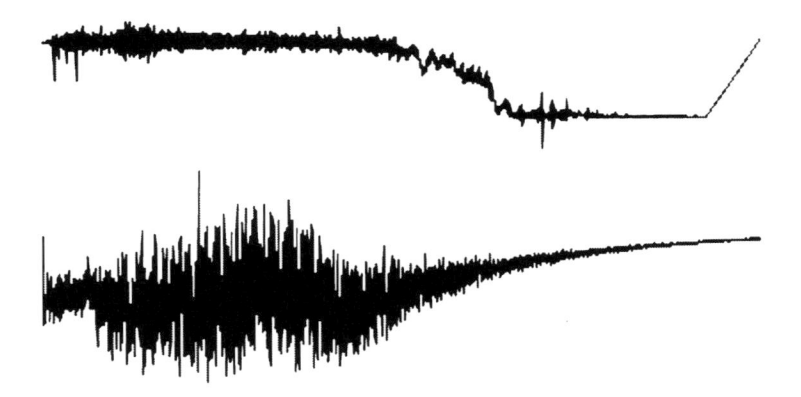

The piercing quality of a unicorn's voice is apparent in these two waveforms with a unmistakable horn-like terminations.

14

Listen for a soft crooning.

> He heard a new sound, very faint and melodic. Singing, perhaps? ... Suddenly the unicorn spoke to him. "Follow the sun," it said in its singsong voice.
> —Mary Kirchoff, *Night of the Eye* (1994)

No matter how softly a unicorn might sing, the voice will permeate the surroundings, as with Tom Waits. Indeed, Jeanie Lemaire speaks of the "very soft but penetrating voice" of the unicorn (*The Body Talks ... and I Can Hear It*, 1996).

Soft crooning may build in energy and intensity. The pagan theorist and peace activist Starhawk describes how "a low crooning, a deep vibration barely heard" manifests into a miraculous unicorn horn. The crooning slowly rises into "an eerie nonharmony. The air seems to thicken, to dance with electric sparks that begin to fly, circle, spin, careen madly." The sonic sparks make the atmosphere glow like a luminous, pulsating cloud. "The light spirals upward, faster, faster, as it narrows toward the top. The sound is indescribable; the voices are the shrieking wind, the howling of wolves, the high cries of tropical birds, the swarming of bees, the sigh of receding waves. The cone builds and builds a pulsing spiral, a unicorn's horn, rare and marvelous" (*The Spiral Dance*, 1979). It's as if the unicorn's singing is at once a conical transmission tower and the audio signal that emanates from it.

A unicorn's crooning may also sound:

- like it's not meant for others to hear
- like a teakettle on the fire
- like a mother's lullaby over a cradle
- low and pulsing, from deep in the throat
- sentimental
- mournful
- tender, affectionate
- emotionally charged
- like the purring of a kitten
- gentle, mellow
- whispery
- voluptuous
- like nonsense syllables
- unforced, spontaneous
- like the texture of buttermilk

Literary accounts of unicorns' soft crooning include:

> He heard a unicorn make a soft crooning noise. He looked around sharply but couldn't see anything.
> —Titanium Ranger, "Ranger Talk" (2006)

> He blew out a soft sound, the way a unicorn mare comforts a foal.
> —Mary Stanton, *Unicorns of Balinor: Valley of Fear* (1999)

Concentrated Sound Energy

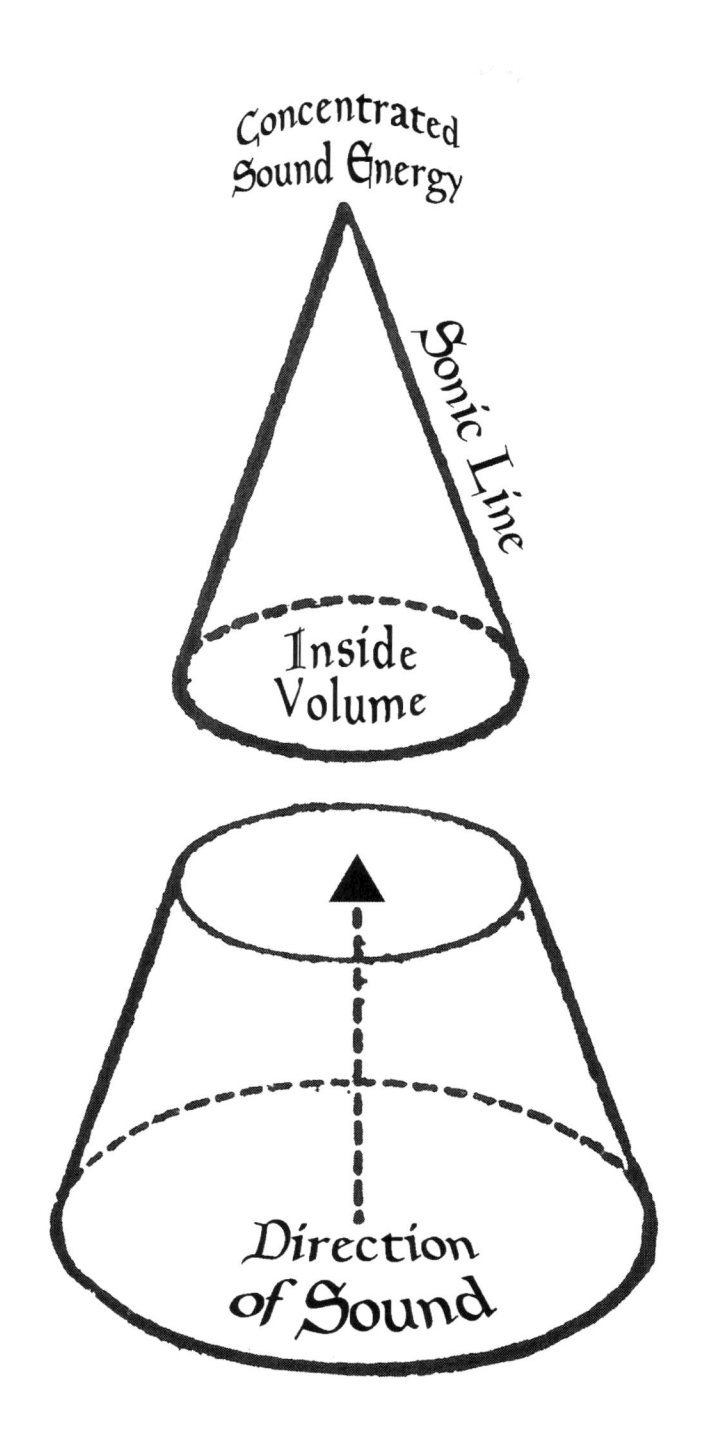

Sonic Line

Inside Volume

Direction of Sound

15

Listen for a calm, gentle voice.

> It speaks in a gentle voice, neither male nor female, its dark eyes twinkling with wisdom.
> —Starfrye, "The Forest of Paths" (2003)

The calm, gentle voice of the unicorn is akin to E.T.A. Hoffman's description of "gentle spirit-voices; the melodies they sang had long lain dormant in my breast, and now they came to life afresh!" (*Kreisleriana*, 1813).

A unicorn's calm, gentle voice can sound:

- like a timeworn prophet's expression of faith
- completely relaxed
- like fine wine
- unemotional
- like a cool drink of water
- soothing
- like the voice of a spirit
- like someone coaxing a shy cat

Accounts of unicorns' calm, gentle voices in literature include:

In a very calm voice (almost hypnotic) the unicorn started conversation with him.
—Terdell Lee Johnson, *The Judges Chronicles* (2004)

"You are the one," spoke the unicorn in a calm, gentle voice, holding strength in every syllable.
—Eric Lafferty, *Over Shadowed Nights* (2002)

"Well, good evening, travelers," said the unicorn in a warm and gentle voice.
—Sheila Brogan, *Fitch on the Road* (2003)

16

Listen for a deep and sonorous baritone.

> "'Tis just as well," the unicorn said, in a deep, sonorous voice, like James Earl Jones playing Mr. Ed.
> —Angela Knight, *Master of the Night* (2004)

Mary Stanton documents a unicorn's powerful, low-pitched, rich and resonant voice in *The Secrets of the Scepter* (2000).

Bear in mind that the lowest calls of a unicorn may be difficult to discern:

> Kellen would have given a lot to know what that conversation consisted of, but the unicorn's voice was pitched too low for him to hear. (Mercedes Lackey, *The Outstretched Shadow*, 2003)

A unicorn's deep, sonorous baritone may sound:

- like an echo in a deep chamber of secrets
- like black velvet

- throaty
- otherworldly
- like a shadow
- caressing
- embracing
- like a foghorn in the mist
- like a ketchup commercial
- hollow
- like the roar of rain-swollen clouds
- like bowling pins toppling, many lanes away
- soul-vibrating
- like a proclamation
- like an ancestral voice
- like rich, dark brandy

The waveform of the low, resonant voice of a unicorn.

Liveliness
100%
80%
60%
40%
20%
0%

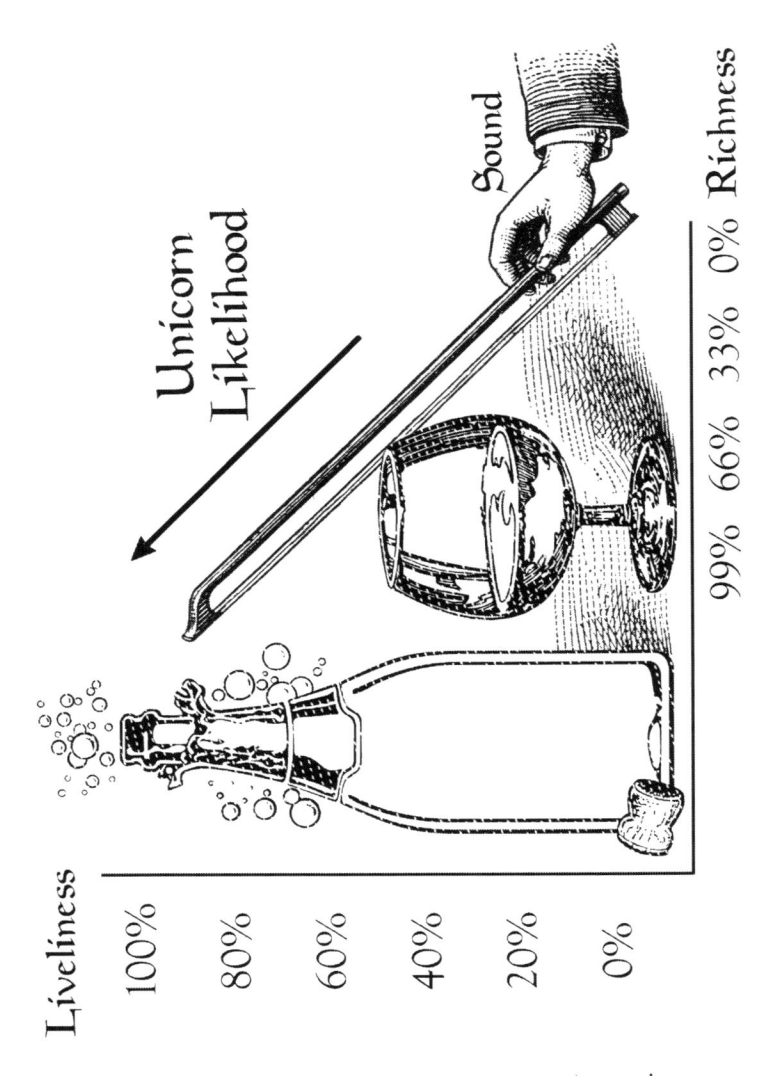

99% 66% 33% 0% Richness

Unicorn Likelihood

Sound

Her voice was rich and dark like good brandy, yet somehow lively too, like the very best champagne.
—George P. Garrett, *The Magic Striptease* (2003)

17

Listen for a playful murmuring.

> The unicorns murmured, and several of them lay down with the abrupt motion of a cat that wants to play.
> —Pamela Dean, *The Secret Country* (2003)

A unicorn's playful murmuring may sound like:

- a mystic's flute
- a small wind rising through the grass
- the babbling of two intersecting brooks
- a form of talk beyond language
- an eerie music box
- a ripple of surprise
- three graduate students drinking coffee

Notice how this waveform of a unicorn's murmuring seems to improvise at the end, playfully galloping off on a new course.

18

Listen for haughty sniffing.

> Vain, haughty, but incredibly beautiful, the unicorn . . . spoke to me.
> —Rita, quoted in *Self-Hypnosis: The Chicago Paradigm* by Stephen Kahn (1990)

Simon Green reports a unicorn's "haughty sniffing" in *Blue Moon Rising* (1991). That said, a unicorn's sniffing is more likely practical than patronizing. A unicorn's capacity for smell can range up to 10,000 different airborne scents, though the precise figure may be influenced by air temperature, altitude, and pH. A short, polite sniff is typically used to reveal fleeting environmental smells. Very occasionally, a unicorn's sniffing will be a manifestation of mild allergies, but this is too rare a phenomenon to concern us here.

Accounts of unicorn sniffing in literature include:

> The unicorns sniffed at them and snorted expressively, but didn't make any hostile moves.
> —Christine Morgan, "Lead Me Not" (1997)

The unicorn sniffed haughtily.
—Craig Shaw Gardner, *A Difficulty with Dwarves* (1987)

The graceful creature took a few steps toward Michael, stretching its head forward, sniffing.
—Bruce Coville, *A Glory of Unicorns* (2000)

The unicorn shook himself off and took a few steps, sniffing the air.
—Mercedes Lackey, *The Outstretched Shadow* (2003)

19

Listen for heavy breathing.

> What is voice? Voice is breath.
> —Hazrat Inayat Khan, *The Mysticism of Sound and Music*

Every time a unicorn exhales, it speaks. Before you dismiss unicorns as long-winded bores, however, you should consider the following insight, from the Indian Sufi master Hazrat Inayat Khan:

> When we study the science of breath, the first thing we notice is that breath is audible; it is a word in itself, for what we call a word is only a more pronounced utterance of breath fashioned by the mouth and tongue. In the capacity of the mouth breath becomes voice, and therefore the original condition of a word is breath. (*The Mysticism of Sound and Music*, 1991)

Resounding at intervals, the magnificent, throaty bursts of unicorn breath can sound like:

- rasping winds from subterranean caverns
- an angry surf
- a buzz saw

- a pair of bellows
- a roaring in one's ears
- a purr
- Velcro opening
- a freight train engine
- thunder
- the furnace cycling on (or, in warm climates, the air conditioner)

The transfixing sound of heavy breathing can indicate the presence of a nearby unicorn, as mentioned by Walter Dean Myers in *Shadow of the Red Moon* (1995). Other accounts of unicorn breathing in literature include:

> The unicorn blew softly through his nostrils and then *spoke!*
> —Dot Taig, *Satylea Scrolls: Lost Soul* (2005)

> He stopped a few feet away, nostrils flaring, breathing heavily.
> —Sunblind, "The Unicorn Herd" (2006)

> The unicorn released a shuddering breath through its nostrils.
> —Jedi Boadicea, "Tears of Fire" (2003)

> The unicorn's voice is breathy, and it reminds you of a breeze in summer.
> —Saebrylla (2006)

Particularly heavy unicorn respiration could indicate "mouth breathing," which means that you may, after all, be dealing with a unicorn subject to nasal congestion as a result of allergies.

Listen for an echoing chant.

> Belief is more
> than listening to the echo
> of the unicorn's voice
> chanting
> as it leaps from mesa to mesa
> above deep chasms in a steep desert valley,
> in search of the griffin
> that guards the egg of the phoenix
> waiting to hatch and emerge
> in flames.
> —Yakov Azriel, "Belief" (2004)

The droning, echoing chants of unicorns transport the listener beyond language, into the hallowed world of pure vibration. The secret to the delightful sound of unicorn chanting is that no two unicorns have exactly the same intonation or vibrato. Their combined frequencies merge to create a smooth, shimmering tapestry of sound.

Uplifting, inspiring, and transcendent, unicorn chants can sound like:

- a message from another world
- high-church hymns

- the sacred OM mantra
- a distant storm
- an endless repetition
- yodelling
- an angelic refrain
- an invocation of a spiritual essence
- divine wisdom
- throat singing
- baseball catcher patter

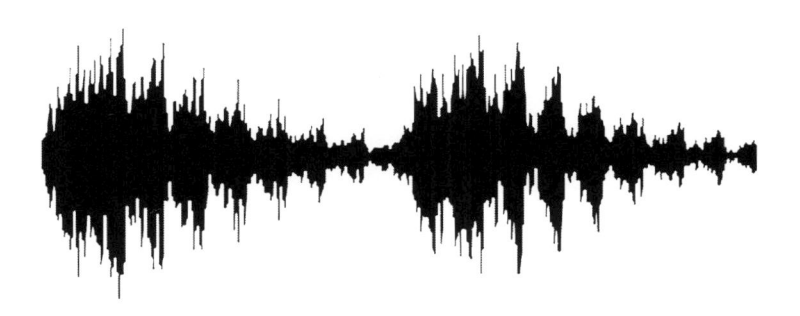

Notice the reverberations in this waveform of a unicorn's echoing chant.

21

Listen for a hoarse rasp.

> The sound of his hoarse voice hung heavy in
> the air like a call from across a great chasm.
> —Robin Jones Gunn, *A Heart Full of Hop*
> (1999)

The hoarse bellow or rasp of a unicorn is said to carry a long distance (Paul A. Johnshard, *Dragons and Unicorns: A Natural History*, 1992).

Emanating from deep within the throat, a unicorn's hoarse rasp may sound:

- like tires crunching over gravel
- like a handsaw cutting wood
- like the howling winds of winter
- like wrinkling foil
- like a Beat poet
- like an old elevator
- coarse
- husky
- guttural
- rough
- low-pitched

- gruff
- gritty
- dissonant
- cough-like
- squeaky
- croaky
- labored and slow

The poet Stephen Dobyns wrote of "the dissonance of unicorns" ("Name-Burning," *Velicities: New and Selected Poems*, 1994). Other accounts of unicorns' rasping voices in literature include:

> The unicorn's voice was hoarse.
> —Mercedes Lackey, *The Outstretched Shadow* (2003)

The waveform of a unicorn's gritty rasp.

22

Listen for strained braying.

> The melancholy braying of the unicorns,
> frightened and despairing, reached them.
> —Walter Myers, *Shadow of the Red Moon* (1995)

On many an occasion, the labored braying of a unicorn has taken a bystander by surprise. That is because the troubled vibrations are like nothing one has ever heard before. Interestingly, a unicorn's braying has the uncanny effect of deepening the quiet in the environment. This is believed to be due to a sonic "interference" effect, whereby the inverted waveform of the braying cancels out more ordinary sound waves.

A unicorn's strained braying may sound:

- like qualmish laughter
- like trumpets
- like howls of derision
- mournful
- hysterical
- loud
- scared

- joyless
- anguished
- jeering
- agitated
- raucous
- dreary
- effortful
- ominous
- booming
- like an automobile horn
- like bagpipes

Accounts of unicorn braying in literature include:

> There was nothing more horible [sic] than the voice or braying of it, for the voice is strained above measure.
> —Rev. Edward Topsell, qtd. in *The Animal-Lore of Shakespeare's Time* by Emma Phipson (1976)

> The unicorn screamed, a high, keening sound like a woman in pain.
> —Harry Turtledove, *Counting Up, Counting Down* (2005)

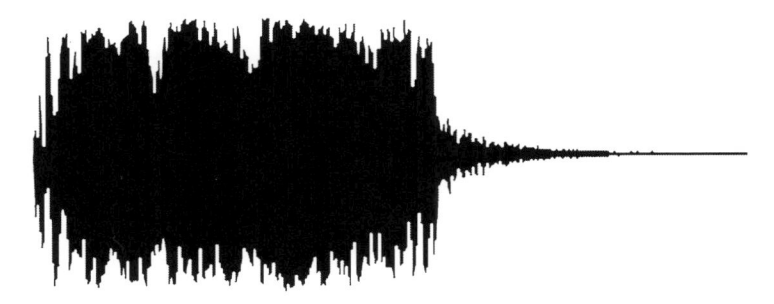

The waveform of a unicorn's strained braying. The flat line on the far right indicates the deep silence that follows.

23

Listen for humdrum humming.

The garden variety call of a unicorn is, by definition, ordinary. As with contemporary classical music, the tones may sound monotonous to the untrained ear. In *To Light a Candle* (2005), Mercedes Lackey describes a unicorn's voice as "bland." The challenge for the listener is to distinguish unicorn humming from other environmental sounds, such as the humming of insect wings. If you hear a loud swarm of bumblebees when no bees are visible, it may be a unicorn.

Accounts of humdrum unicorn humming in literature include:

> Whispering behind him sounded like the humming of insects: unimportant, beneath his notice. He did not hear the words spoken. Whisper of footsteps, and the unicorn lifted its head.
> —Lara Bartram, "Once In a Lullaby" (2004)

Note the "monotonous" regularity is this waveform of a unicorn's humming.

24

Listen for foreign phrases.

Given their prominence in Medieval Europe, it comes as no surprise that some unicorns speak impeccable Latin:

> "In truth," the telepathic beast answers in precise Latin and with a human timbre, more clearly than its voice has ever sounded before. "I am transfigured!" (A. A. Attanasio, *The Dragon and the Unicorn*, 1996)

One colorful report describes a unicorn speaking an Esperantoesque mélange of languages:

> The white unicorn snorted and tossed his head again. In a language that sounded like a mixture of Spanish and Italian with a touch of Dutch, he spoke, "I do not like to be kept waiting. There are better things I could be doing" (Tassana Burrfoot, "The Time of Change," 2006).

25

Listen for weary, forlorn cries.

> The unicorn sounded utterly weary.
> —Mercedes Lackey, *The Outstretched Shadow* (2003)

After a spell of prolonged activity, a unicorn's voice is likely to betray weariness.

A unicorn's forlorn cry may sound:

- like a prophecy
- woebegone
- melodramatic

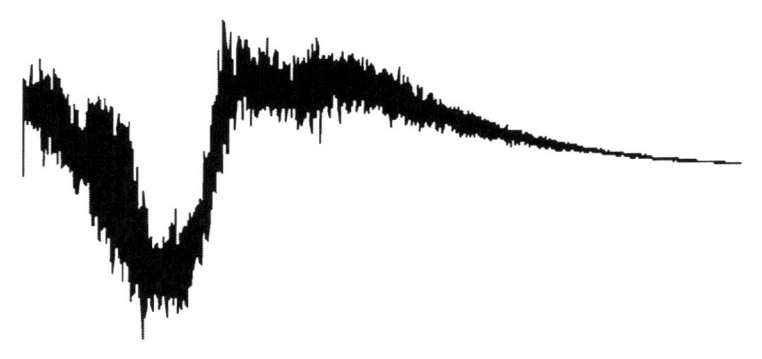

Notice the emotional roller coaster apparent in this waveform of a unicorn's forlorn cry.

- like a death knell
- like an apology
- like a requiem
- like a child up past bedtime
- abandoned
- like a mixture of groans and sighs
- like a Yoko Ono record

Accounts of unicorns' weary cries in literature include:

> Awful groans came from the unicorn, such sounds as are not heard in the fields we know.
> —Lord Dunsany, *The King of Elfland's Daughter* (1924)

Cricothyroid muscle

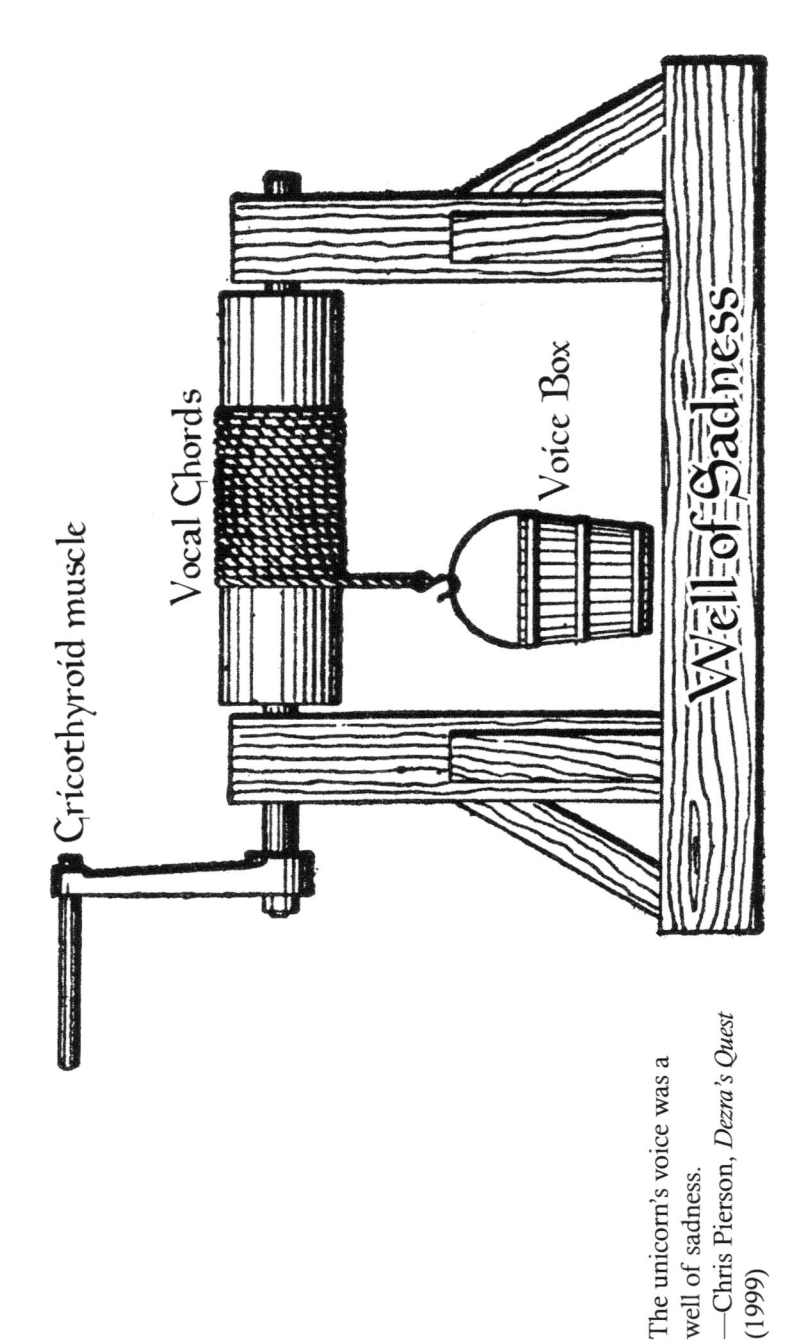

Vocal Chords

Voice Box

Well of Sadness

The unicorn's voice was a well of sadness.
—Chris Pierson, *Dezra's Quest* (1999)

26

Listen for a magical sound.

> Discovering Magic means recognizing the
> illusory nature of the material world.
> —Phillip Cooper, *Esoteric Magic and the Cabala*
> (2002)

The mysterious, magical utterances of unicorns have incomparable power to fascinate, excite, and enchant. The word *magic* "evokes childhood memories of fireflies dancing in the dark, of fairies living in the garden; of dreams being so real they lapse over into waking time. We blew the fizz off dandelions in order to have wishes come true, or wished upon the first rising star. We breathed in magic and were not at all surprised by the wonders we encountered" (Galen Gillotte, *Sacred Stones of the Goddess*, 2003).

The ethereal, magical voice of a unicorn tends to unfold like a flower captured by time-lapse photography, its sweet melody swirling around the listener like a beautiful fragrance. It can also sound like:

- crumpled silk
- an expression of gratitude

- a soft, primitive incantation
- humming high-tension wires
- an otherworldly harp
- a menu item that is unavailable this evening
- a stone dropping into a quiet pool
- dream-like remembrances
- an entire forest of songbirds
- the ringing of a crystal bowl
- a pinwheel
- a stereo that has been powered up but on which nothing is being played

Accounts of unicorns' magical sounds in literature include:

> The breeze had gone, the air was still
> just silence echoed all around
> and then as if in a dream,
> It raised its head and made a sound totally unlike a whinny.
> —Gina L. Dartt, "Unicorn" (2006)

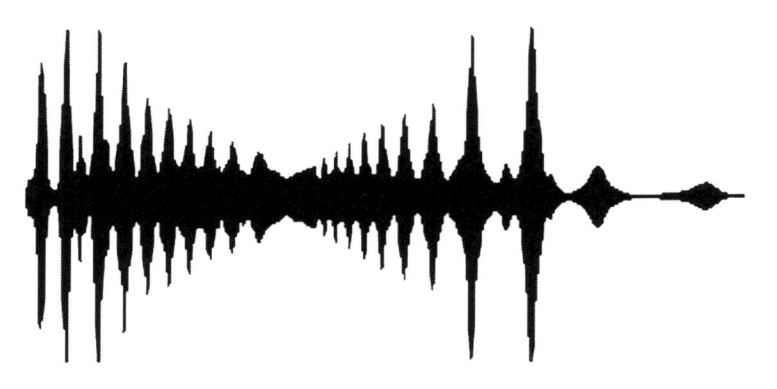

In this waveform of magical unicorn sounds, notice the unusual vibrational symmetry.

I heard a sound behind me, a gentle rustling
as of leaves or silk, though there was no wind,
and I spun about again to see what marvellous
creature might appear.
—Tom Harper, *The Mosaic of Shadows* (2005)

I heard it, the most magical sound.
From the water, a magical creature appeared
—Rebecca Harris, "The Wizard Man" (2004)

Then the unicorn spoke in a magical, musical
voice. "Open the window, Claire. Come for a
ride on my back."
—Guy Inchbald, "The Jigsaw Unicorn"
(2001)

I can't remember exactly what it sounded like,
but his voice was very beautiful.
—Josephine, "Diana and the Unicorn" (2004)

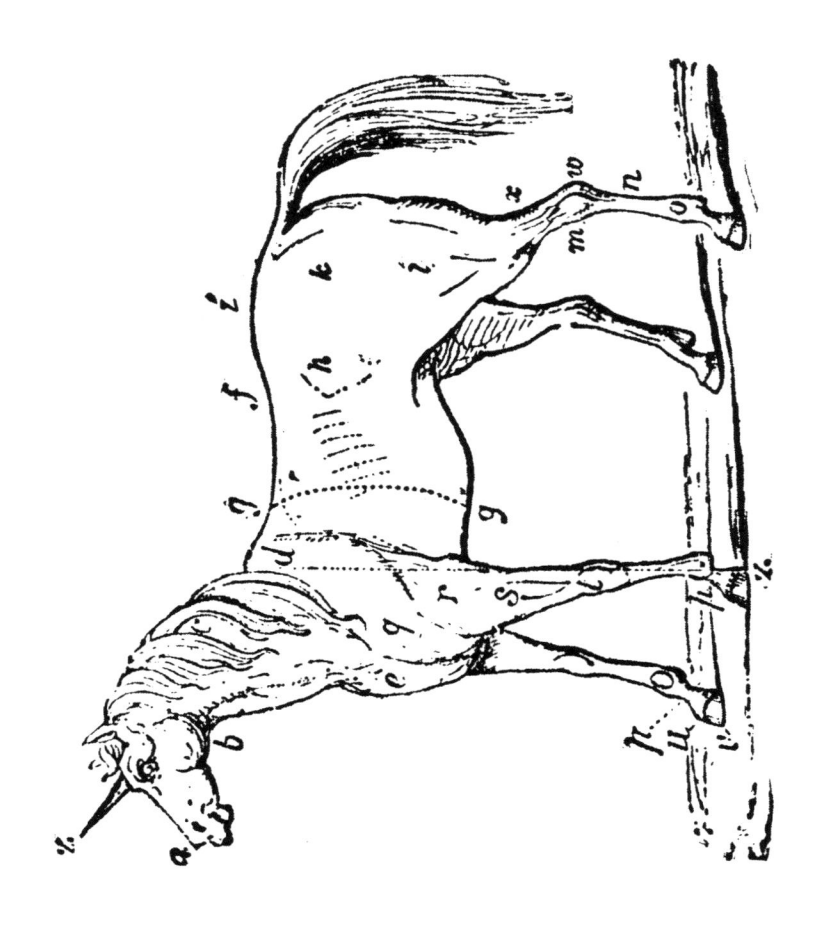

Mystics from time immemorial have believed the alphabet to encapsulate divine creative power. This illustration from the late 1800's shows how the entire alphabet is crystallized in a unicorn's body. It's little wonder, then, that unicorns are such miraculous communicators.

92

27

Listen for a terrible cry of ruin.

> With an old, gay, terrible cry of ruin, the
> unicorn reared out of her hiding place.
> —Peter Beagle, *The Last Unicorn* (1968)

When on the run from pursuers, a unicorn may sound as if it is falling to pieces.

In the eighth century, St. John Damascene described a rampant unicorn's "terrible bellowing" that was beyond human endurance (*Barlaam and Loasaph*). Other accounts of unicorns' ruinous cries in literature include:

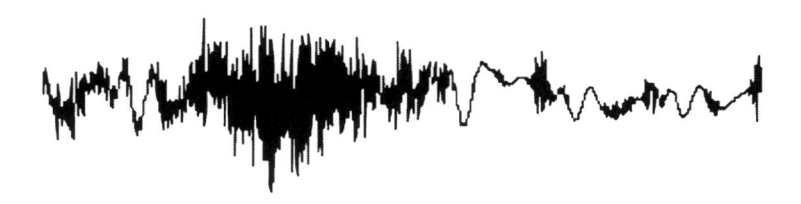

In this waveform of a unicorn's ruinous cry, the sound grows haphazard and literally breaks down at the end.

a hoof steps out amongst the trees,
a silver mane flows in the breeze
an elegant neck strains up to the sky,
as a unicorn gives a curdling cry
—Cerridwen, "The Unicorn's Blood" (2006)

28

Listen for a soft growling.

> And the unicorn growls softly, very softly, so as not to frighten them. The crowd gapes with wonder.
> —Peter Spielberg, *Twiddledum Twaddledum* (1974)

A unicorn's extraordinary soft growling is oddly mesmerizing, like the purring of a guinea pig. The sound's hypnotic quality makes it difficult to pinpoint in space, however, even with state-of-the-art equipment. The dreamlike growl tends to smooth out and even obliterate other environmental sounds.

The waveform of a unicorn's affectionate growling.

29

Listen for a lilting voice.

The pulsing intonation of a unicorn's voice is described in *The Whim of the Dragon* by Pamela Dean (2003). This captivating, lightsome voice may sound like:

- a wondrous cascading
- an exotic lullaby
- something out of a fairy tale
- a strange, melodic chuckling
- a trickling flute
- a comfort
- a mourning dove
- an angelic shower
- a happy cooing

The waveform of a unicorn's lilting voice clearly displays a cadence.

- Ella Fitzgerald
- spiritually-charged vibrations
- burbling water
- something from the future
- peculiarly clear

Though soft and sweet, one may shiver to hear it.

30

Listen for a baby's bleating call.

Sometimes disconcerting, always unforgettable, the abrupt bleating call of a baby unicorn may sound like:

- a groaning hinge
- the crying of doomed spirits
- a trembling plea for help
- a sacrificial lamb
- a military camp bugle
- an officious duck
- an assistant manager

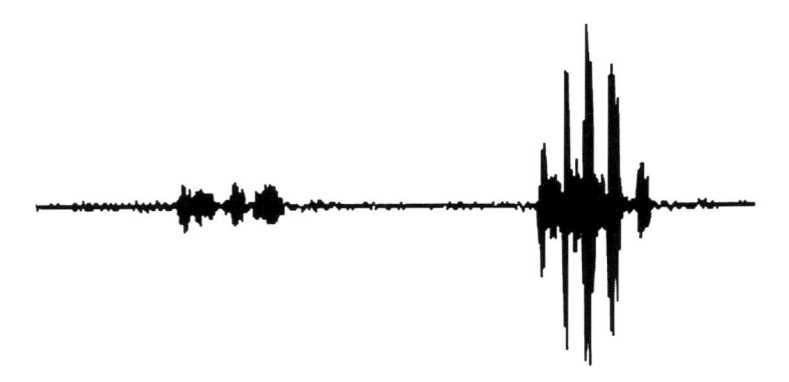

The waveform of a mother unicorn's "contact call" (left) and her baby's answering bleat (right).

Accounts of unicorn babies' bleating calls in literature include:

> Babies have a soft, bleating call with which they answer their mother's "contact call." This contact call is used by the mother to reassure her fawn and keep it informed of her location, even when they are fairly close together.
> —Paul A. Johnshard, *Dragons and Unicorns: A Natural History* (1992)

31

Listen for a quivering neigh.

The slightly trembling voice of a unicorn is documented by Jean Thesman in her book entitled *Between* (2002).

Quivering neighs can sound like:

- a prayer for forgiveness
- strings of a harp drawn by a passing wind
- frailty
- unearthly fluting
- the flourish of a distant trumpet

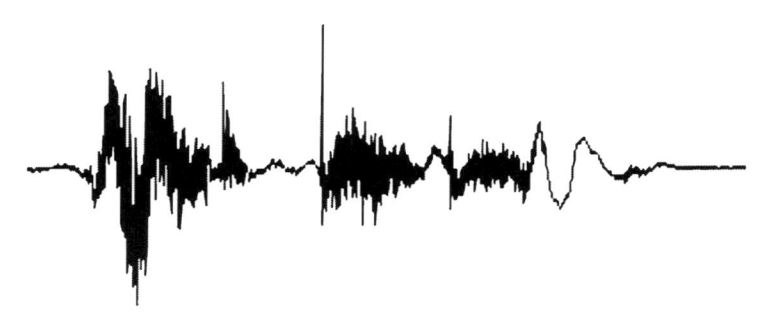

Notice the trembling apparent in this waveform of a unicorn's quivering neigh.

Accounts of unicorns' quivering neighs in literature include:

> A unicorn neighed; I folded
>   His neck in my arms
> And was safe, as he lay down,
> All night, from thickening Heaven.
> —James Dickey, "Chenille," *The Whole Motion* (1992)

32

Listen for cascading glissandi.

In musical terminology, a glissando is a continuous slide upward or downward between two notes. A police siren is an example of a glissando. Though only cascading glissandi have been recorded in the field, a unicorn's soaring glissando is theoretically possible.

A glissando can sound like:

- an otherworldly halo
- a liquescent mystery
- a blurred leap
- a siren's song
- an eerie keening

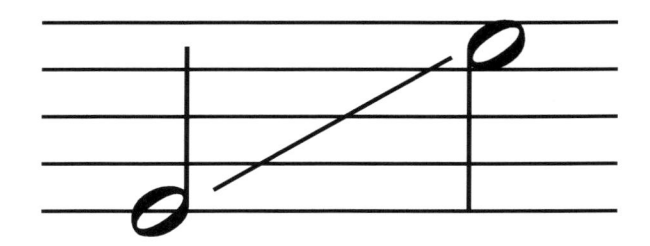

The musical notation for a glissando.

- a celestial blessing
- a bizarre growl
- a slow percolation
- a relic of an unknown sound spectrum
- a piece of wizardry
- a "wolf whistle"

Accounts of unicorns' cascading glissandi in literature include:

> He shone in the moonlight, his voice warm as sunshine, and his eyes clear sky blue. He sang to [them] with amusement. . . . His grand song arched over them, cascading glissandos of starlight notes forming a rainbow road on which they galloped over the treetops.
> —Conrad Wong, "Chasing Unicorn Songs" (1990)

33

Listen for proud neighing.

> They were lost to the eye, even when the prancing of their feet and their proud neighings still reached the ear.
> —William Pickering, *Incidents of the Apostolic Age in Britain* (1844)

A unicorn's proud neighing can sound:

- triumphant
- reassuring
- vainglorious
- presumptuous
- theatric

The waveform of a unicorn's proud neighing. The bold swelling at the end of the sound reveals the beast's confidence.

- atavistic
- lofty
- stubborn
- fantastical
- regal
- flowery
- heroic

Accounts of unicorns' proud neighing in literature include:

> Neighing proudly, it threw back its flawless mane.
> —Brendan Walsh, *Tales from the War* (2003)

34

Listen for gentle snorting.

> Snorting and ramping, the unicorn came leading the grand march.
> —Charles Finney, *The Circus of Dr. Lao* (1935)

In *Blue Moon Rising* (1991), Simon Green documents the snorting sound of a unicorn. As Mercedes Lackey explains in *The Outstretched Shadow* (2004), unicorns have "expressive nostrils."

A unicorn's gentle snorting can sound:

- like contained laughter
- impatient
- critical
- friendly
- inviting
- like a choking cough
- dismissive
- contented
- cautiously optimistic
- like a gleeful assertion
- hungry
- startled

- deep
- dubious

Note that even a gentle snort may betray fear:

> The black unicorn snorted, an indelicate, frightened sound, and the shadows of the wood seemed to shimmer in response. (Terry Brooks, *The Black Unicorn*, 1987)

Accounts of unicorns' gentle snorting in literature include:

> A loud neighing followed by a snort came from Nightwind's right. Around the side of the knoll came several unicorns.
> —William Kyle, *Return from Legend* (2004)

> The unicorn's tail flicked, and its ears twitched. It snorted a few times.
> —Carla Jablonski, *The Books of Magic: Consequences* (2004)

> The unicorn snorted gently.
> —Mercedes Lackey, *To Light a Candle* (2005)

35

Listen for the bellowing wail of a mating call.

During the breeding period in mid-September, male unicorns "begin to seek out mature females by periodic calling. The calls are heard during early morning and late evening hours. The voice of the male unicorn has usually been described as a loud wail. Other than during breeding season, unicorns are surprisingly silent and as a result are extremely hard to find" (Paul A. Johnshard, *Dragons and Unicorns: A Natural History*, 1992).

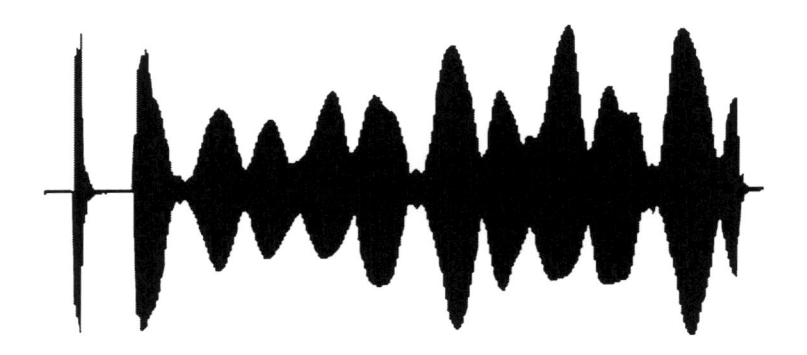

The waveform of a unicorn's mating bellow.

36

Listen for the crunch of dry pine needles.

> Then the Unicorn stamped the ground with his hoof, and shook his mane, and spoke.
> —C.S. Lewis, *The Chronicles of Narnia: The Last Battle* (1956)

Leave those "needles in a haystack" behind and turn your ear toward unicorns in a bed of pine needles. The crunch of fallen pine needles can be a dead giveaway that a unicorn is present. As unicorns stamp and paw the ground, the crisp leaves beneath them will crackle:

> The dry pine needles crumbled beneath her feet and the unicorns' hooves, scenting the still night air. (Kathleen Duey, *The Mountains of the Moon*, 2002)

It would seem that unicorns are especially fond of galloping amongst pine trees, no doubt lured by the scented air.

Unicorn hoof/Pine Needle Crunch Waveform

Silence

Displacement

Pine Needle

2 Cycles

Unicorn hoof

Autumnal Foliage

37

Listen for an alarm "sneeze."

Accounts of unicorns' alarm sneezes in literature include:

> When alarmed, resting unicorns utter a small sneezelike sound that alerts other nearby unicorns to possible danger; this is especially true of mothers guarding their fawns. On hearing such a sneeze, the fawn will lower its head and fold its ears back, so that it becomes almost invisible in the grass, and it remains thus until its hidden mother calls to it.
> —Paul A. Johnshard, *Dragons and Unicorns: A Natural History* (1992)

It is not necessary to say "Gesundheit" to unicorns.

Notice the sudden expulsion at the end of this waveform of a unicorn's alarm "sneeze."

Listen for a deafening peal of thunder.

> The unicorn roared in a voice of thunder.
> —Kathy "Nightstar" Garrison, "Unicorn Lost" (2004)

At its loudest, a unicorn's roar resembles:

- a thunderclap through Alpine crags
- a roaring locomotive
- a waterfall
- the crashing of immense ocean waves
- cannon fire
- an avalanche of boulders
- a hundred kettledrums
- an earthquake
- a cracking glacier
- an erupting volcano

Such a howl is as thrilling as it is frightful. Depending upon the unicorn, the blast may sound:

- ominous
- oracular

- wrathful
- boisterous
- melodious
- enthusiastic
- everlasting

Accounts of unicorns' thunderous peals in literature include:

> It was as though a thousand horses were neighing and screaming all at once. Fritz's heart stood still. He wanted to run away, but his legs refused to move. As he stood there, shaking and quaking, there rushed out of the forest a huge unicorn with a spiral golden horn on his forehead. "What seek you here?" asked the unicorn, in a voice of thunder.
> —Nora Archibald Smith, *Tales of Wonder* (1909)

> There was a deafening sound, a loud throbbing cry as from the breast of a plangent unicorn.
> —Bosevo, *44 Rue D'Assas* (2000)

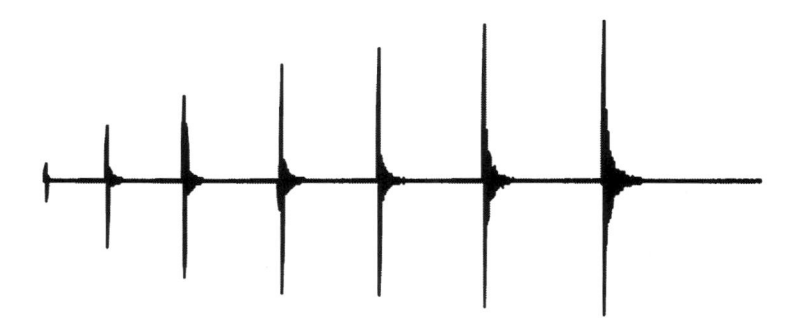

Like a resounding kettledrum, a unicorn's thunderous peal gets progressively louder in this dramatic waveform.

39

Listen for a heart-touching sound.

> The Unicorn's call touched his heart.
> —Julie Winningham, "The Books of the Unicorn" (2001)

The heart-touching sound of a unicorn can be:

- harmonious
- sweet and clear
- soft, yet firm
- affectionate
- delicate as a butterfly
- spontaneous
- innocent as a child
- devotional

The waveform of a unicorn's heart-touching voice.

- joyous
- breathtaking
- barely perceptible
- emotionally manipulative
- pleading
- thankful

Accounts of unicorns' heart-touching voices in literature include:

> I listen with my Heart,
> To hear you when you call.
> 'Tis the voice of the Unicorn,
> It teaches—Love is all.
> —John Van Horn, "I Believe in Unicorns" (2006)

46

Listen for a splash of water.

> Water cascaded down heaving flanks, and the unicorn shook his mane, water droplets flying like ice.
> —Alice L. Raven, "Down By the Sea" (2005)

Whether for drinking, cleaning, playing, or contemplating, unicorns love water.

Accounts of unicorns' water splashing in literature include:

> Halo spoke with a voice that sounded as beautiful and pure as the sweet trickling of fresh spring water. "We feel as though we know you all so well after watching you for so many years."
> —Jasper Cooper, *Cassandra's Gift* (2006)

> The murmuring of fountains mingles with the neighing of unicorns. You shall hear them; and the face of the Unknown shall be unveiled!
> —Gustave Flaubert, *The Temptation of Saint Anthony* (1874)

The two girls heard the unicorns coming long before they saw them—a wild, rushing sound, like surf across pebbles.
—Katherine Roberts, *Spellfall* (2003)

Listen for a dreadful, tree-shaking shriek of rage.

> Way out nowhere with a pair of enraged unicorns!
> —Piers Anthony, *Being a Green Mother* (1987)

You might believe the whole earth was trembling. For a moment, you might believe the world was coming to an end. When "driven beyond endurance," a unicorn may "scream a cry of rage" so dreadful that it can affect the sanity of an aggressor (Lair2000, "Dragon Facts," 2000). The thunderous, deafening, devouring shriek is indeed bone-rattling and tree-shaking. It sounds like the announcement of an earthquake or a furious whirlwind. From a great distance, the shriek sounds like white noise filling the entire sky.

Accounts of unicorns' enraged shrieks in literature include:

> The unicorn screamed, and the scream sounded like that of a man.
> —Josephine, "Diana and the Unicorn" (2004)

Rearing into the air to blot out the center sun, the unicorn let out a wail that shook the distant trees.
—Keith Michael Mahan, *Dragon Isle* (2004)

The unicorn bellowed, its sound joining with the woman's scream.
—Jack Yeovil, *Genevieve Undead* (2002)

The waveform of a unicorn's enraged shriek. Note how a series of aftershocks in the middle lead to a fresh round of thunder.

42

Listen for a harsh braying.

> Abruptly, a harsh braying broke the idyll. Alcy leaped into the air, barely avoiding a herd of charging unicorns.
> —Willow Skye Robinson, *Prince of New Avon* (2004)

Like a war trumpet, a unicorn's harsh bray conveys no warmth. Grating on the ears, harsh braying can sound:

- discordant
- like a grating bark
- not so much angry as disappointed
- alarming
- bossy
- raspy
- like guffaws of laughter
- shrill, piercing
- tense
- crazed
- ragged
- rattling
- tormented
- grievous

- like feedback blasting from a microphone loop
- like a bowstring on the verge of snapping
- like an outboard boat motor
- like a donkey's final bellow

43

Listen for a ruffling sound.

> A ruffling cascade, like a stack of ladies' fans sliding silkily off a credenza.
> —Gregory Maguire, *Son of a Witch* (2006)

The ruffling sounds of a unicorn are reminiscent of:

- the feathers of a settling peacock
- a pillow being fluffed
- riffling through the pages of an enormous dictionary
- the rippling of a boat's sail
- the gentle shoveling of fresh popcorn into a bucket
- a breeze whispering through leafy treetops or a field of grass on a mild summer's day
- a pigeon fidgeting on a windowsill
- a bedsheet being shaken

The waveform of a unicorn's ruffling sound.

- a curtain being pulled back
- unfurling scrolls of small waves

Accounts of unicorns' ruffling sounds in literature include:

> It had come through a gap in the trees, magical in the twilight, the colour of the dusk, and put its damp nose down and sniffed at Flora and made a soft ruffling sound.
> —John Roe, *All This Is So: A Future History* (2004)

44

Listen for a soft nicker.

> The unicorn nickered and walked forward.
> —Gwen Perkins, "The Hunt" (2006)

A nicker is produced when a unicorn uses its vocal chords to create a vibrating sound with its mouth closed. The technique is similar to that practiced by ventriloquists, but unicorns usually achieve less vulgar results.

A unicorn's gentle nicker can indicate recognition and express pleasure. It can also be questioning:

> Something made a questioning sound out in the brush, and he looked up warily. Glowing yellow eyes looked at him before their owner vanished with a rustle. (Angela Knight, *Master of the Night*, 2004)

Soft nickers can also sound:

- comforting
- beckoning
- like a low chuckle
- contented

- almost musical
- approving
- guttural
- pulsating
- rapid-fire
- soothing
- plaintive
- encouraging
- mellow
- purposeful
- soporific

Accounts of unicorns' soft nickers in literature include:

> A soft nicker and a prickly muzzle pushed in her face. . . . As her eyes adjusted to the darkness, Jade saw many white shapes lying around and she realized she was in the midst of the unicorn herd.
> —Shawn Snead, *Dragon's Egg* (2002)

> The unicorn hesitated. Its long, tufted tail swished indecisively. Tilting its head to one side in a quizzical manner, it nickered through its long nose.
> —Ayinsan, "Pleasant Days: Twin" (2003)

The vibratory waveform of a unicorn's soft nicker.

45

Listen for a breathy whinny.

> If I close my eyes and listen, sometimes, I can hear a far-off whinny that seems to drag me towards it.
> —Mythriss, "More Unicorn Moments" (2006)

When a unicorn whinnies, it lets its breath out in little bursts. Squeals of light "laughter" are not uncommon at the beginning of a whinny. A sort of moaning sound at the end is typical. Rich with overtones and building in energy to a climax, a breathy whinny can sound like:

- a juicy secret
- a quiet orgasm

Accounts of unicorns' breathy whinnies in literature include:

> The unicorn whickered welcome.
> —*Peter Beagle's Immortal Unicorn* (1995)

> The unicorn made a whinny, and pawed again with his hoof.
> —T. H. White, *Once and Future King* (1958)

Listen for a slumberous sigh.

> The Unicorn sighed sentimentally.
> —Richard Harding Davis, *The Lion and the Unicorn* (1899)

Unicorns are prone to sighing when overcome by sudden drowsiness or melancholy. A slumberous sigh can sound:

- like a wave breaking very slowly
- half-forlorn
- immense
- sensuous
- pensive
- involuntary
- sumptuous
- nostalgic

The waveform of a unicorn's slumberous sigh.

47

Listen for the clicking of kicked-up hooves.

> A white unicorn was kicking up its hooves in the middle of a green-and-red field.
> —Joy Fielding, *See Jane Run* (1991)

Clang. Clank. Clink. Clatter. From a distance, the kicked-up hooves of unicorns sounds like the clinking of doubloons or flutes of champagne.

Note, however, that depending upon environmental conditions, the clicking of hooves can be quite subtle or even imperceptible. Bruce Coville records that "The unicorns' silver hooves made no sound at all (*A Glory of Unicorns*, 2000). Similarly, we have this report from Mercedes Lackey and John Mallory:

> Shalkan's hooves made no sound at all as the unicorn trotted over the surface of the snow. (*When Darkness Falls*, 2006)

Accounts of unicorns clicking their kicked-up hooves in literature include:

The unicorn kicked up his back hooves and sprang into motion.
—Magpie Poet, "Slaughter of Innocents" (2002)

He kicked up his hooves and came trotting, slowly at first, but steadily gaining speed, until finally he was galloping faster than the wind.
—Margaret Mayo, *Mystical Birds And Beasts From Many Lands* (1997)

48

Listen for the sounds of grazing.

> The sound is unbearably close, and I think I might know what it is. Yes, it's a young unicorn chomping on grass.
> —T. L. Welch, *Terra Splendora* (2006)

Unicorn grazing can sound:

- peaceful
- contented
- ruminative
- monotonous
- delicate
- careful
- serene

Accounts of unicorns' grazing sounds in literature include:

> [It was a] unicorn nibbling noisily on a patch of crabgrass.
> —Jennifer N. Julian, "Quests: Part III" (2003)

Neither of us moved as we regarded the apparition: a soft, shimmering white encompassed it, as if it were covered with down rather than fur and maning; its tiny, cloven hooves were golden, as was the delicate, whorled horn that rose from its narrow head. It stood atop one of the lesser rocks, nibbling at the lichen that grew there. Its eyes, when it raised them and looked in our direction, were a bright, emerald green. It joined us in immobility for a pair of instants. Then it made a quick, nervous gesture with its front feet, pawing the air and striking the stone, three times. And then it blurred and vanished like a snowflake, silently, perhaps in the woods to our right.
—Roger Zelanzy, *Sign of the Unicorn* (1975)

Advanced Practice

*I can truthfully tell you that it is
a blessing to talk with a unicorn.*
—N. J. W. Mitchell,
Hannah, the Witch, and the Unicorn (2002)

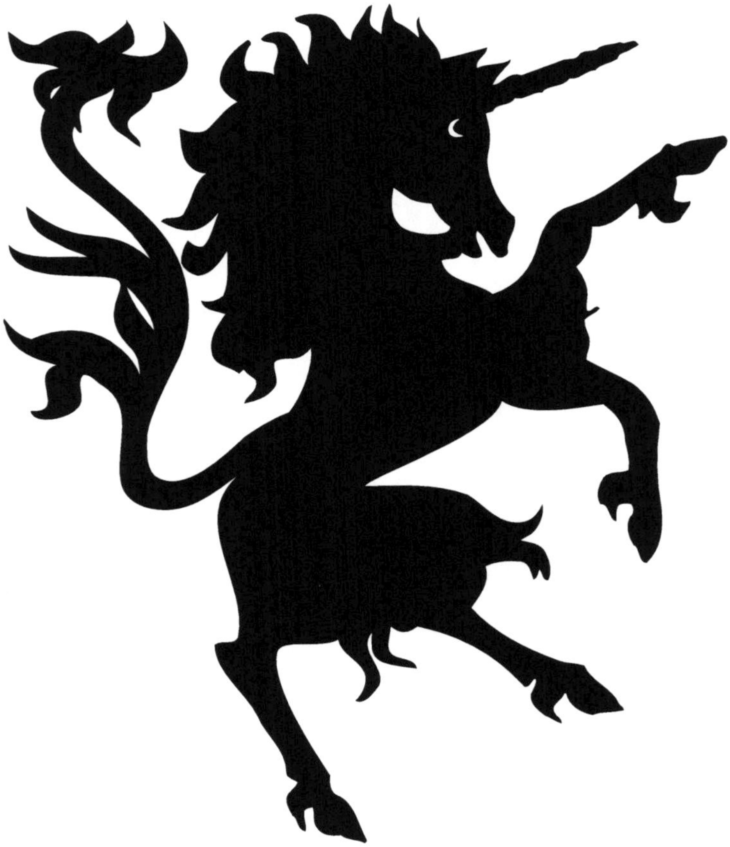

Listen for singing whistles.

The singing whistles of a unicorn are difficult to distinguish from birdsong. Experienced birdwatchers will have an easier time detecting these high-pitched sounds made when a unicorn forces air through its teeth or partly closed lips. The effect is not unlike that of the powerful whistling sound used by Manhattan doormen to summon taxicabs.

In *Inheritance of a Sword and a Path* (2005), Douglas Van Dyke Jr. refers to unicorn language as the "whistle-song." He describes herd leaders making distinctive calls "like a variety of whistles set in a musical tone." He goes on to explain how the leaders use these whistles to guide a herd in motion:

> The noise was very different than anything that a horse might utter. Unicorns did give voice to a distinctive variety of singing whistles to communicate with each other. The herd leaders, which were always matriarchs, used the whistle-song to guide the rest of their followers.... The echoes of the song trilled and reverberated as it guided the direction of a hundred sets of unicorn hooves.... [T]he herd ... switched directions on the run, flowing one way then striking a new direction

as the leaders whistled out directions. It was much akin to the way flocks of birds and schools of fish changed direction, seemingly on impulse, sending the whole group in a new direction as one.

Listen for breathless silence.

> Then, the unicorn stilled, all was silent again.
> A breath, a sigh, a salute.
> —Bosevo, *44 Rue D'Assas* (2000)

"When you expect an event to occur, your brain is highly sensitized to that possibility," suggests Dr. Katya Rubia of France's national Institute of Psychiatry. Hearing expert Pierre Fonlupt of the Inserm institute explains: "The auditory cortex is activated when a subject is attending to and listening to silence, when expecting an upcoming sound" (BBC News, 2004).

To sensitize your brain to notice unicorn sounds, take special notice of silence, which is available locally in many areas. Focus on the spaces between sounds. Here are some things to practice listening for, as suggested by New Zealand naturalist Pete McGregor in his essay "Sounds and Silence" (2006):

- a fumbling and buzzing bumble bee settling onto a blue clothes peg
- a lone swallow swooping past without a sound

- the soft rattle of cabbage tree leaves ceasing when the wind dies down
- a far-off airplane flying behind the clouds
- the soft rustle of long grass dislodging the weight of old rain, then resuming quiet contentment
- a bird singing silence (some notes and phrases are beyond our range of hearing)

Be aware that listening to silence can be a profound experience. Silence takes us beyond the ordinary. In his essay "The Sound of Silence" (2003), Thomas Váczy Hightower recalls his first encounter with silence: "Standing by the inland ice, I heard for the first time the sound of silence. It nearly struck me to the ground, so strong was the pressure."

Accounts of unicorn silence in literature include:

> The Unicorn watched, but made never a sound.
> —Joe Nigg, *Wonder Beasts: Tales and Lore of the Phoenix, the Griffin, the Unicorn, and the Dragon* (1995)

> Without sound the unicorn is suddenly there in a forest clearing.
> —Jennifer Lash, *Blood Ties* (1999)

> It was a unicorn. Silence fell.
> —Pamela Freeman, *The Centre of Magic* (1998)

> The unicorn stands in silence, not once gesturing or mentally communicating with me.
> —David Santana, *Journey to the Mythological Realm* (2003)

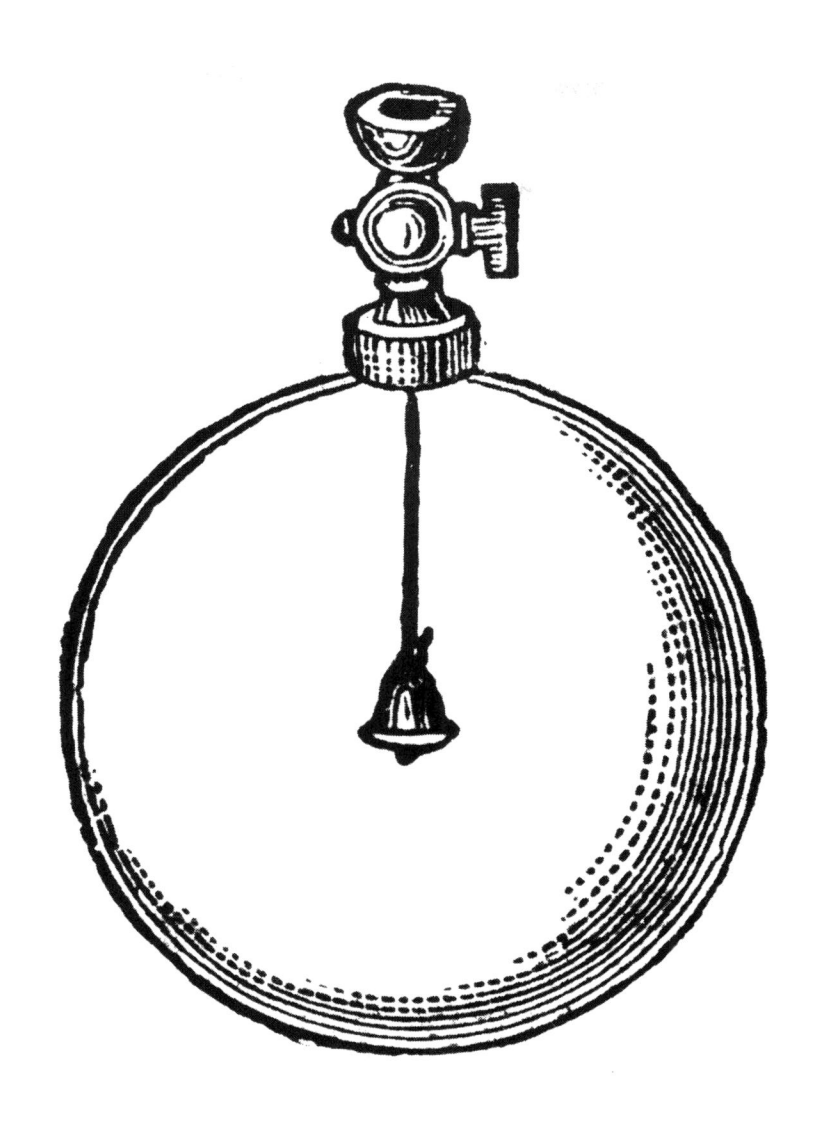

What is the sound of unicorn silence? Imagine a tiny bell, jingling inside a thick glass bulb. (How in the world did they get the bell in there?)

He listened. Listened for a noise he hadn't heard. There was no rustle in the tall grasses in the field behind. There was no call of birds as they soared in a breath of wind high above. Not even the wind dared to breathe. The silence was unnerving.
—Sheona R. McCaig, *Scrolls of Power* (2003)

It was while she was standing silently, her head tilted as she tried to understand what a silver birch was saying, that the unicorn came.
—Pamela Freeman, *The Willow Tree's Daughter* (1994)

The unicorn was silent for a while.
—Geoffrey Grosshans, *Likely Stories* (2004)

Then the sight of the unicorn forced them into a silence that was oddly reverent.
—*Peter Beagle's Immortal Unicorn* (1995)

Across the clearing, the unicorn, silent, immobile, seemed to watch.
—Tanith Lee, *Red Unicorn* (1998)

The Unicorn dared not make a sound.
—John Dent-Young (trans.), *The Gathering Company* (2001)

The unicorn only looked at her without making a sound.
—Dellwyn Oseana, *Xunitopia: The Search for Imagination* (2005)

Unicorn Silence: Reversing the Vicious Cycle

Natural unicorn quietude is a wondrous thing. But an unnatural hush has come over unicorn populations around the world. A "culture of silence" disseminates the misinformation that unicorns don't exist, thereby perpetuating a vicious cycle. Something natural goes into hiding, essentially becoming invisible. Unicorns' needs are hidden and go unrecognized, thus perpetuating poor public policy and fueling the culture of silence. The diagram above* shows how the vicious cycle can be broken.

* Inspired by Quality Education for Social Transformation, "Reversing the Cycle of Silence" (2001)

Listen to deeper layers.

Calm your mind, focus your awareness, and practice listening to deeper and deeper layers of sound.

- 1st Layer
    ordinary wildlife around you (the calls and rustling of birds, insects, small animals)

- 2nd Layer
    the elements (the whispers of the wind, the splashes of water, the tumbling of stones)

- 3rd Layer
    your own breathing or footsteps

- 4th Layer
    your own heartbeat (or wristwatch)

. . .

- nth Layer
    the vibrations of a frolicking unicorn

> The unicorn's electricity hummed through me, and in my brain the blossoms of heaven opened.
> —A. Attanasio, *The Dragon & the Unicorn* (1996)

Appendix: Unicorn Sound Levels in Decibels

120	Thunderclap roar
118	Shriek of rage
116	Cry of ruin
114	Strained or harsh braying
112	Mating wail
110	Weary cry
105	Baby's bleating
100	Musical cry
90	Sonorous baritone
80	Proud neighing
75	Quivering neigh
70	Joyful laughter
65	Clip-clop gallop
60	Clicking of kicked-up hooves
55	Hoarse rasp
50	Gentle snorting
45	Alarm sneeze
40	Splash of water
38	Soft nicker
36	Breathy whinny
34	Soft growl
32	Lilting, gentle voice
30	Soft crooning
29	Cascading glissandos
28	Tranquil sound
27	Playful murmuring
26	Humdrum humming
25	Faint humming
24	Haughty sniff
23	Grazing
22	Ruffling or rustling
20	Heavy breathing
10	Slumberous sigh
5	Faint wind chime
0	Sound of falling snow
-	Breathless silence
-	Magical sound
-	Telepathic communication

Printed in Great Britain
by Amazon